"Is that why you agreed to help your father this summer—so you two could mend your fences?"

"Yes." A soft sigh escaped her. "But that was when I believed I was his only child."

"You are his only child."

"You might not be his son by birth, but it's obvious he cares more about you than me."

The truth was painful.

Rachel stepped past Clint, but he grasped her hand. His warm, callused fingers entwined with hers, sending shivers racing along her arm.

"This isn't a competition between us," he said.

Who was Clint kidding? They'd have to wait until the end of the summer to see which one of them came out on top in her father's eyes.

Dear Reader,

While writing my cowboy books for Harlequin American Romance, I occasionally stumble across information about women's rough-stock events, but usually never pay much attention to the details. After all, the average American woman has little in common with a female bull rider—right? Wrong. On a whim I began to research these courageous, spirited cowgirls and realized they're more like you and me than I'd first believed. Whether women work in education, health care, business, are stay-at-home moms raising children or even romance writers, they face obstacles in the workplace and at home that most men don't. Each and every day, women fight for recognition, respect, equal pay and equal benefits. When women fail, they pick themselves up, dust off their Wranglers and return for another go-round the next day.

I can't think of a better example of bravery, dedication and resilience than a cowgirl who competes in rough-stock events. I hope you find inspiration from these courageous women and enjoy the wild world of rodeo!

For more information on my books and my Rodeo Rebels series for Harlequin American Romance, visit my website, www.marinthomas.com.

Happy reading!

Marin

Arizona Cowboy

MARIN THOMAS

HARLEQUIN®

entertain, enrich, inspire™

Recycling programs
for this product may
not exist in your area.

ISBN-13: 978-0-373-75487-8

ARIZONA COWBOY

www.Harlequin.com

Printed in U.S.A.

ABOUT THE AUTHOR

Marin Thomas grew up in Janesville, Wisconsin. She left the Midwest to attend college in Tucson, Arizona, where she earned a B.A. in radio-TV. Following graduation she married her college sweetheart in a five-minute ceremony at the historic Little Chapel of the West in Las Vegas, Nevada. Over the years she and her family have lived in seven different states, but they've now come full circle and returned to Arizona, where the rugged desert and breathtaking sunsets provide plenty of inspiration for Marin's cowboy books.

Books by Marin Thomas

HARLEQUIN AMERICAN ROMANCE

  *The McKade Brothers
 **Hearts of Appalachia
***Rodeo Rebels

To all the cowgirls who dare to dream big!

Chapter One

Stagecoach 10 Miles

Rachel Lewis strangled the steering wheel Sunday afternoon as she sped along the deserted Arizona highway southeast of Yuma. Although she'd been born in this desolate wasteland, the bone-dry landscape remained unfamiliar to her. The car's thermometer displayed 100—it was only June seventh. After living two decades in Rhode Island, temps over eighty degrees constituted *sweltering.*

How did people survive this heat? Better yet...how would *she* handle three months of hundred-degree-plus temperatures on her father's ranch?

You're almost there. Eight hours in her car and the wavy heat lines hovering above the baking asphalt threatened to mesmerize Rachel. She gulped several swallows from her water bottle. Her concentration restored, she searched for a large rock, a mountain peak, a saguaro with too many arms—anything that might help her recall the first few years of her life in Hell's backyard. *Nothing.* She felt like a tourist in a foreign land.

When Rachel was five years old, her mother had died in a horse accident and her father had shipped Rachel east to live with her aunt. Twenty-two years later she was returning to her birthplace—not because she wanted to but because her father had asked her to.

The speedometer nudged eighty and she eased her foot off the accelerator. Thoughts of P. T. Lewis sent her blood pressure soaring. A week before the public schools in Rhode Island had dismissed for the summer Rachel had learned her father had been diagnosed with prostate cancer and would be undergoing three months of treatment at a medical center in Phoenix. Before she'd uttered a single word of sympathy, he'd asked her to return to Stagecoach to run his rodeo-production company.

The phone call had been the first time her father had reached out to her since her mother's death and the hurt, abandoned little girl in Rachel had yearned to shout, "No!"

But Rachel wasn't a child. She was a grown woman with a successful career as a high school psychologist and athletic trainer. On a daily basis she dealt with teenagers who struggled with anger-management issues, eating disorders, physical disabilities and social adjustment problems. Too bad her background in psychology did nothing to ease the anger and hurt that had festered inside her the past twenty-two years. Her immature reaction to her father's request had triggered a bout of serious soul-searching.

Deep down she yearned to be needed by her father because he loved her—not because he wanted her to manage his business. Dare she hope P.T.'s call for help signaled a desire to mend their relationship? After several sleepless nights Rachel had acknowledged she wasn't certain she was able or even willing to forgive her father for choosing not to be involved in her life. In the end, his health had convinced her to attempt reconciliation.

P.T. was all the family Rachel had left, but she hesitated about becoming too close to him when a chance existed that he wouldn't beat his cancer. All these years she'd struggled to accept her father's disregard. If she opened her heart to him and then he didn't survive… How would she endure losing her father twice in one lifetime?

I wish you were here to help me, Aunt Edith.

Rachel loved her aunt for all the sacrifices

the woman had made in raising Rachel. Aunt Edith was the sole reason Rachel had survived her father's absence through the years. Her aunt had never openly criticized her brother for neglecting his only child, but Rachel had eavesdropped on phone conversations through the years and overheard Aunt Edith reprimand her brother for not visiting Rachel or speaking with her on the phone.

Relax. It's not as if you're going to a job interview. She might as well be. For all intents and purposes, P.T. was a stranger to her.

Turn around and go home. Say you changed your mind. Not after driving over twenty-five hundred miles and crossing thirteen states in three and a half days.

Needing to mentally prepare herself for seeing her father, Rachel had chosen to drive rather than fly to Arizona. The last meeting with P.T. had been at her aunt's funeral two years ago. He'd stayed one night at a hotel then departed the following morning.

The road curved around an outcropping of jagged rock and Rachel focused on her driving. After executing the turn, she had a split second to react to the roadblock in her lane. She slammed her foot on the brake, wincing as the seat belt bit into her skin. Fear of crashing into the rock wall on her right or skidding off the shoulder on her left prevented Rachel from swerving. She squeezed her eyes closed then sent a silent prayer heavenward.

Screeching tires on asphalt filled Rachel's ears and the smell of burning rubber spewed from the air-conditioning vents. Not more than a few seconds had passed before the car rocked to a halt. Fingers fused to the steering wheel, it took a moment for her to realize she hadn't hit the big, brown blob. Relieved, she exhaled and opened her eyes.

Oh...my...God. Was that a bull drooling on the hood of her silver Prius? She scanned the horizon. Where was a cowboy when you needed one?

Rachel laid on the horn but instead of moving, the stubborn animal blew snot on her windshield. "It's going to be like that, is it?" She should put the car in Reverse, then drove past the ugly beast, but she couldn't take the chance that another vehicle might hit the animal. Intent on coaxing the bull off the road, she set the parking brake and got out. Keeping the driver-side door between her and the bull, she waved her hands in the air. "Git! Scoot!"

A stare down ensued.

While Rachel contemplated her next move, a horn blasted in the distance. Shielding her gaze from the afternoon sun, she spotted a truck barreling along a rocky incline, kicking up a dust storm that would put a tornado to shame. The driver skillfully maneuvered the vehicle through a maze of rocks and prickly pear cacti before stopping at the edge of the road. He leaped from the truck. "You didn't hit him, did you?"

Ignoring his question, she asked, "Does this dumb animal belong to you?"

The cowboy was older than Rachel by a few years. Lines bracketed his mouth and fanned from the corners of his eyes, attesting to a life working in the desert. A little over six feet, his broad shoulders hinted at plenty of muscle beneath his long-sleeved blue cotton shirt. Rachel doubted there was a woman on earth who wouldn't feel protected and safe with this man's arms wrapped around her.

He stopped next to the bull and bent at the waist, flashing his sexy backside at her. The Wrangler jeans fit his tight… She cleared her throat, miffed that the cowboy appeared more concerned with the bull than her. "Aren't you going to ask if I'm all right?"

His brown-eyed gaze traveled over her body. "You don't appear as shaken as Curly."

How would he know if the bull was upset or not? "*Curly* looks fine to me."

"The tire's resting on his hoof."

"Oh, no!" Forgetting her safety, Rachel rushed to the front of the car only to discover the tire was nowhere near the bull's hoof. "Your sense of humor stinks, mister."

He grinned and Rachel's heart jolted. His crooked smile highlighted a sexy dimple in his cheek and gorgeous teeth, which appeared unnaturally white against his tanned face. Stuck in cowboy-ogle land, Rachel gaped.

"Sorry." He removed his Stetson and scratched his head. "Couldn't resist teasing you." He wore his dark hair neatly trimmed— the no-nonsense style at odds with the twinkle in his brown eyes.

"You've been out in the sun too long and the heat has baked your brain." Rachel perched her hands on her hips. "Are you going to move this bull off the road?"

"That depends."

"On what?"

"Well, ma'am, if you have a gadget in your car I can use to…"

After he'd called her *ma'am* Rachel hadn't heard a word he'd said. "How old do you think I am?"

"Pardon?"

"You called me ma'am."

There went his grin again…stealing the oxygen from her lungs. "We cowboys use that term loosely."

Irritated by his cocky attitude she said, "I'm twenty-seven."

"Yes, ma'am."

Good grief. She glanced at her watch. "How long is this going to take?"

"Curly's stubborn. He won't budge until he's good 'n' ready."

"If the bull is that difficult why isn't he contained behind a fence?"

"Mating season." The man's cheeks turned ruddy. "Every so often Curly succumbs to nature's call and busts through the fence to get to his girlfriend."

Males and their damned urges. "Sounds like Curly needs an owner who's smarter than him."

Her barb didn't faze him. "Like I said before, Curly's—"

"Stubborn." So was Rachel. She pushed the cowboy out of her way then shoved the bull's rump with both hands. The big nuisance turned his head and stared at her.

The cowboy smirked.

"Least you could do is help," Rachel snapped.

His grin widened.

"Maybe Curly needs a little encouragement." She hopped into the driver's seat and started the engine, swallowing a chuckle when the cowboy's mouth sagged open. Rachel shifted into Drive, then slowly—very slowly—lifted her foot off the brake. The car rocked forward, bumping the bull's side. The beast didn't move. She pressed the tip of her toe against the gas but the bull stood solid. Frustrated, she laid on the horn. Curly didn't bat an eyelash but the cowboy almost jumped out of his boots.

As far as Clint was concerned the uppity lady had no sense of humor. He should have guessed as much by the car she drove—one of them silly hybrids. Shoot, she was probably a vegetarian because beef came from cattle and bovines polluted the air with methane gas. Even so, she had the most beautiful mouth—when it wasn't sassing him. Full lips painted with a sparkly pink gloss that begged for a man's kiss.

He walked to the driver's side and waited for her to lower the window. "You got a fly swatter or an umbrella?" He had plenty of gizmos in his truck but he wasn't in a rush to go anywhere.

"What do you need…never mind." She shut off the car then leaned over the front seat and rummaged through a shopping bag on the floor, offering Clint a bird's-eye view of her firm fanny.

Too bad the lady was so uptight or he might be interested in learning her final destination. He hadn't seen a ring on her finger but he'd noticed plenty more. A large clip secured a mass of wavy blond hair to her head. Several strands escaped the sexy pile, softening her face. Khaki shorts showed off pale legs—toned in all the right places—and a sleeveless shirt hugged her small breasts. He wished she'd take off her sunglasses so he could see the color of her eyes. It had been a long while since he'd come upon a woman who'd snagged his interest. A shame she was a snoot.

"Here it is." She produced a plastic back scratcher painted to resemble a saguaro cactus. She'd probably purchased the cheesy souvenir at one of several tourist stands scattered along the highway.

"That'll work." His fingers bumped hers when he grabbed the scratcher, and a warm sensation shot up his arm. He attributed his reaction to the female dry spell he was experiencing. He'd lost track of when he and Monica had parted ways—must have been months ago if his body found a prissy woman in a Prius attractive.

"Need help?" she asked, getting out of the car.

"No. Stand back."

"What do you plan to do?" She retreated half a step. "Scratch Curly's back until he moves off the road?"

You don't know the half of it, lady. Not wishing to offend her feminine sensibilities, Clint said, "Wait behind the car."

"I doubt whacking that bull on the butt will make him aggressive." She did an about-face and retreated.

"I'm not whacking him. I'm tickling Curly."

"What nonsense. If there was a blasted cell tower somewhere in this desert I'd contact the highway patrol."

Clint patted Curly's head. "You've heard of horse whisperers, haven't you? Bull-whispering isn't much different." He chuckled as he moved the scratcher along Curly's flank…lower over the bull's stomach…backward toward his testicles… He heard a gasp but remained focused in case the bull kicked out.

"Are you doing what I think you're doing?" she asked.

"Yes, ma'am."

"That's disgusting."

"You want Curly to move out of the way or not?"

"I don't see how scratching his you-know-whats is going to—"

Right then Curly swung his massive head and bellowed. A second later he stood on his hind legs and slammed his front hooves onto the hood of the car. A short scream followed by a strangled gasp accompanied Curly's grunts.

As soon as the bull found relief, he backed away from the Prius, leaving his hoof prints embedded in the car.

"Go on home, Curly!" The sated bull trotted into the desert, following the same path Clint had taken to reach the road. Satisfied the bull was headed to the ranch, Clint turned his attention to the woman in a stunned stupor.

"If you give me your name and number I'll make arrangements with my insurance company to pay to have the dents pounded out of the hood."

"Never mind."

Clint fished his wallet from his back pocket and removed a business card. "If you change your—"

"I won't." She hopped into the front seat and shut the door.

Keeping a straight face he held out the plastic souvenir. "You forgot your back scratcher."

Rachel hit the gas and sped off. She checked the rearview mirror and caught the cowboy tipping his hat to her. "Of all the nerve..." The arrogant man hadn't even apologized for the trouble his sex-crazed bull had caused.

If all Arizona had to offer was horny bulls and worthless cowboys then maybe her father had done her a favor when he'd banished her to the East Coast to live with her aunt. Oh, who was she kidding? Males were the same everywhere. Her ex-fiancé had taught her that men were only loyal to their own wants and needs.

Her thoughts shifted to P.T. He'd never remarried after her mother had passed away. What kind of woman would she have become if she'd been raised on a ranch by a single father? More likely than not Rachel would have grown up a tomboy and become a *cowgirl.* The image made her shudder.

She studied the scrubby landscape racing past the car window. The hostile desert appeared forbidding and forlorn. The cowboy had probably befriended *Curly* to avoid going insane with loneliness.

Stagecoach, Arizona
Playground of Butch Cassidy and the
Sundance Kid

THROUGH THE YEARS, Aunt Edith had regaled her with stories about her birthplace in an attempt to help Rachel bond with P.T. If her father had shown the slightest interest in being an involved parent she might have listened more closely to her aunt's tales.

One mile later, Rachel slowed the car as she

entered the town of Stagecoach, thirty-five miles southeast of Yuma. The main drag consisted of four blocks of businesses, stucco ranch homes and double-wide trailers. Landscaping was nonexistent, save for the thorny weeds that sprouted from dirt yards. Rachel counted three bars—nothing better to do than drink when scorching temperatures forced you inside during the day.

She drove past Mel's Barber Shop and the Bee Luv Lee Beauty Salon. Rachel searched for places to eat—José's Mexican Diner, Burger Hut and Vern's Drive-In. An antiques business sat across the street from José's, the front yard crowded with junk. Rachel pulled into a Chevron gas station advertising dollar hot dogs and a free coffee with a fill up. She topped off the tank and ran the car through the wash, then passed a Wells Fargo Savings and Loan on the way out of town.

Rachel increased the volume on her GPS and waited for Australian Karen's next commands. The down-under voice instructed Rachel to turn left onto Star Road, which led to her father's home—Five Star Ranch. The Prius bumped along the gravel path and she cursed the orange dust that stuck to the still-wet car. When she reached the top of a hill she applied the brakes and lowered the window. The desert-scented air failed to trigger a memory of the barn and corrals shaded by mesquite trees.

Five Star Ranch was a rough-stock sanctuary where retired rodeo broncs and bulls grazed away their remaining years. Rachel had difficulty reconciling the man who'd given her away with the man who possessed a soft spot for the fierce athletic animals.

Tears burned her eyes and she wiped angrily at her cheeks. P.T. didn't deserve tears. She closed the window and drove on. She knew next to nothing about rodeos or producing one, but P.T. had assured her that she only needed to make a few phone calls to keep the business running. If the task were that simple, why wasn't the ranch foreman assigned the responsibility?

Her stomach clenched as she contemplated her father's motive in bringing her to Arizona. Was his cancer more advanced than he'd let on? Was her visit a final goodbye? No matter P.T.'s reasons, Rachel intended to prove she was capable of handling his company. After the final rodeo in August she'd return to Rhode Island with a clear conscience, knowing she'd helped her father when he hadn't deserved any consideration from her.

Rachel parked in the ranch yard, but kept the car running as she studied the hacienda-style adobe home with Santa Fe accents. The cream-colored structure sported a clay-tiled roof and there appeared to be an enclosed courtyard at the rear of the home. Brown beams protruded near the top of the exterior, suggesting the wood extended throughout the home, providing structural support. The front door had been stained to match the beams.

She perused the yard—if one could call gravel and dirt a yard. She tried to envision herself as a five-year-old playing next to the two giant saguaro cacti—one with a rotting arm. The other was filled with holes—birds' nests. Paloverde trees in various stages of growth provided mottled shade, and a black cat sat next to a large succulent, its swishing tail sending puffs of dust into the air.

That her father owned a nice home and over two-hundred-fifty acres of scrubland didn't surprise her. P.T. had sent Aunt Edith a handsome monthly sum to care for Rachel as well as paying Rachel's college tuition. *Guilt money.* P.T. hadn't deserted Rachel financially—just emotionally.

The front door opened and P.T.'s shadow darkened the entryway. She hadn't expected to be greeted with balloons or party streamers but a smile would have been welcome.

"Here goes nothing." She shut off the car engine and got out. Halfway up the stone path her father stepped outside. P.T. appeared slimmer than she'd remembered from her aunt's funeral. His large gut had shrunk and his broad shoulders caved in toward his chest. His once-dark-gold hair was saturated with gray. P. T. Lewis looked...old. Older than his fifty-six years.

Someone had to speak first. "Hello, Dad."

"Rachel." He motioned to the Prius. "Do you need help with your luggage?"

"No, thanks," she said. Her father wasn't in any shape to tote heavy suitcases.

"Your trip was uneventful, I hope?"

"Pretty much." *Except for Curly and an ill-humored cowboy.*

"C'mon inside. I doubt you remember the place."

Like he'd done twenty-two years ago, Phillip Todd Lewis turned his back on her and walked away.

Chapter Two

"Lauren, you home?" Silence greeted Clint's question when he stepped into the foreman's house at Five Star Ranch. He had a hunch this was going to be the longest summer on record if he and his daughter didn't come to an understanding. Until recently he hadn't played an active role in the eighteen-year-old's life. After he'd gotten Lauren's mother, Liz, pregnant, he'd proposed but she'd declined, preferring to take care of Lauren on her own in California.

He wished he and Lauren had gotten off to a better start when she'd arrived at the ranch two weeks ago. Through the years his bimonthly phone calls to his daughter had been quick and non-informative and his visits with her in Los Angeles had fallen short of his expectations. Instead of spending quality time together he'd chaperoned his daughter and her friends at Disneyland, a shopping mall or the beach.

When Liz had asked if Lauren could spend

the summer with him while she honeymooned in Mexico with her fifth husband, Clint hadn't hesitated. He'd hoped he and his daughter would grow closer—that is, if he could coax Lauren out of her bedroom. She considered her stay at Five Star Ranch a jail sentence and was determined to make Clint as miserable as she was.

Speaking of miserable, Clint couldn't help thinking of the sassy woman he'd rescued Curly from a short while ago. The lady's fiery spirit amused him and he doubted he'd forget those sleek, sexy legs of hers anytime soon. Clint had kicked himself all the way back to the ranch for forgetting to check the car's license plate—not that it would have mattered, but he wanted to know if the blonde lived in the area.

Shoving thoughts of the pretty bull-hater aside, he guzzled a water bottle from the fridge, then strolled down the hallway off the kitchen. He rapped his knuckles against his daughter's door. "Can I come in?"

No answer.

Eyes closed he prayed for patience—a virtue in short supply since he'd learned of P.T.'s cancer diagnosis. The older man's health weighed heavily on Clint's mind. He hated not being able to fight P.T.'s cancer for him but would do his damnedest to make sure the summer rodeos went on as scheduled while P.T. received medical treatment in Phoenix.

"I'm coming in." Clint knocked on the door a second time, then counted to ten before stepping into the room. Lauren was sprawled across the bed, with iPod headphones stuck in her ears. He waved his arm to catch her attention.

"What?" she snapped.

"Did you do the chores on the list I left in the kitchen?" Simple chores—scrubbing the toilet and straightening the bathroom. There wasn't an inch of available counter space for his razor or aftershave. Lauren had claimed the bathroom as her own, forcing Clint to stow his toiletries on the top of his bedroom dresser.

"I didn't see a list."

Hadn't she left her room all day? Maybe she was ill. He approached the bed and placed his palm against her forehead.

"Don't touch me."

"Just checking for a fever."

"I'm not sick." She glared. "I'm bored."

"There's plenty to do on the ranch if you'll haul your keister out of bed." He'd offered to teach Lauren how to feed the livestock, muck the barn and ride a horse, but she'd turned him down.

"It's too hot outside."

Not much he could do about the heat—summer months in Southwest Arizona were hotter than Hades. "The laundry hasn't been done in a while."

"I'm not your slave!" Lauren's nostrils flared.

Wishing he had more experience handling rebellious teenagers, Clint was forced to wing it with his daughter. "Want to see a movie tonight?"

"No."

Clint had risen earlier than usual the past few days. He worked his butt off, even skipping lunch to free up time to be with Lauren in the evenings. So far she'd evaded his attempts to bond with her. "What would you like to do?"

"Drive back to California."

"Sorry, kiddo. No can do."

"I hate it when you do that."

"Do what?" Clint had a hell of a time following the female train of thought.

"Talk to me like I'm twelve."

Huh?

"Why did Mom have to get married again?" Lauren crushed the pillow to her mouth and released a muffled scream.

Lauren had grown up with stepfathers entering and leaving her life in short intervals, but Clint suspected she resented him most. He was her biological father, yet he'd never been there for her. This summer he hoped to make up for his absence in her life, but Lauren appeared intent on sabotaging his efforts.

"You might feel better if you eat." His daughter was small in stature and too slim for his liking.

"I'm not hungry."

"Maybe you'll be hungry in an hour. I've got to check in with P.T., then afterward we'll drive into town for supper."

P.T. had asked Clint to stop by the main house to discuss a few business details. He expected P.T. to officially hand over the reins of his rodeo-production company to him before checking into the Phoenix cancer clinic tomorrow. The income from Five Star Rodeos paid for the feed and care of the retired rough stock, and P.T. worried about the company failing to bring in enough money to support the sanctuary ranch.

"I'm tired of eating out." Lauren's whining returned Clint's focus to the present.

"We'll drive into Yuma and grab a handful of microwavable meals at the grocery store."

"Mmm…tasty." Lauren curled her nose.

His daughter wouldn't give an inch. "Want to buy ingredients and make a meal from scratch?"

"No." She swung her legs over the side of the bed. "I'll get up if you stop badgering me."

Clint backed out of the room and made it

halfway down the hall before Lauren shouted, "Dad!"

As much as he didn't deserve it, he liked hearing his daughter call him Dad. He returned to the doorway. "What?"

"I didn't want to spend the summer before my senior year of high school stuck in the middle of a desert." Angry tears shimmered in Lauren's eyes.

"I'm sorry things didn't work out the way you wanted." Although Lauren had become an adult a month ago, the apartment she shared with her mother wasn't in the safest area of L.A., and he and Liz agreed that the best place for Lauren this summer was at the ranch.

Hoping to goad his daughter into a better mood, he said, "I'll pay to have your hair done while we're in Yuma."

"No one's touching my hair."

When Clint had fetched Lauren in L.A., his jaw had dropped to the ground at the sight of her neon-pink hair and piercings—a silver hoop in her eyebrow and a fake-diamond stud in her nose. Deciding the best course of action was *no comment,* he retreated to the kitchen and washed the previous days' dishes left in the sink.

"If I drive into Yuma with you, I want a Caramel Frappuccino at Starbucks," Lauren said from the kitchen doorway.

Didn't his daughter own a pair of shorts longer than two inches? He studied her outfit, careful to keep his expression neutral. At least her T-shirt wasn't ripped or torn. "Did you pack any jeans this summer?"

"Only stupid people wear long pants when it's over a hundred degrees."

"Are you calling your father stupid?"

Eye roll. "You know what I mean." Lauren helped herself to a bottle of apple juice in the fridge, then sat at the table and stared into space.

Clint dried the dishes, wondering if he and his daughter would ever have a conversation that didn't turn into an argument. They'd bickered more in the past two weeks than they had the past eighteen years. He glanced at the wall clock. He had a few minutes to blow before his chat with P.T. "Have you decided what you want to do after you graduate from high school?"

"Most of my friends are going off to universities or enrolling in community colleges."

Clint joined her at the table.

"I'd like to go away to college. Maybe study green technology."

Whoa. Where had that come from? The term

green technology brought back memories of the pretty blonde Curly had tangled with.

"My chemistry teacher, Mrs. Benton, taught a unit on cutting-edge technology. She said lots of jobs in the future are going to be tied to green energy."

"Sounds interesting." And way over Clint's head.

"Mrs. Benton said green jobs pay well."

"You're a smart girl." His comment erased the frown line across Lauren's forehead.

"You think so?"

Why did she act surprised? "You'll be successful at whatever career you choose."

She opened her mouth then snapped it shut.

"What?"

"Mom said you don't like to talk about your childhood."

"She's right, I don't." Clint had lost count of the foster homes he'd been raised in—some decent, but most best forgotten.

"How come you didn't go to college?" she asked.

"Got sidetracked by rodeo." Because P.T. owned a rodeo-production company, Clint had taken a liking to the sport. Rodeo had given Clint a worthy goal to focus on and a way to put the pain of a lonely childhood behind him and find his own identity.

"Mom said you rode bulls."

Hadn't he discussed his rodeo days with Lauren? He and his daughter really were strangers. "I rode a few broncs, but mostly bulls."

"Did you get injured a lot?"

"Enough." Clint wiggled the crooked pinkie on his left hand. He neglected to tell Lauren that he'd continued to compete with the broken finger and as a result the bone had never healed properly.

"Cowboys who rodeo are crazy."

"Teens who dye their hair neon-pink are crazy." The comment tugged a smile from his daughter.

"Why'd you quit rodeo?" she asked.

"Got too old." Thirty was old by rodeo standards. "After I retired from competing, I became a bullfighter."

"What's that?"

Happy Lauren appeared interested in his past, Clint looked for ways to draw out the discussion. "A bullfighter protects a fallen cowboy by distracting the bull."

"Isn't that dangerous?"

"Yep, but in all the years I worked as a bullfighter I only got gored once."

"Was it bad?"

"Split my thigh from knee to hip. Luckily, the wound wasn't deep." Afterward, P.T. had convinced Clint to quit bullfighting and become the official foreman of Five Star Ranch. By then, Clint had been more than ready to retire his bright-colored jersey, shorts and socks.

"The worst injury I ever suffered was a sprained ankle during badminton practice. I had to use crutches for a week before I could put weight on my foot."

"Sprains can be tricky." Neither Liz nor Lauren had shared that incident with Clint. How many other events in his daughter's life had he never known about? He headed for the door. "I'd better go. P.T.'s waiting."

"Is P.T. okay?"

"He's fine." Lauren knew about the old man's cancer and felt sorry for him. Clint was relieved that beneath his daughter's disgruntled, unhappy exterior resided a sympathetic heart. "P.T. wants to discuss the summer's rodeo schedule."

Lauren sat straighter in the chair. "Does this mean I have to go to the rodeos with you?"

"Looks that way." Clint grabbed his hat from the hook by the back door.

"Cool."

Her comment brought Clint up short. "I thought you couldn't stand cowboys and ranching."

"Some of the cowboys are cute."

Even though his gut insisted his wayward

daughter wasn't a virgin, the last thing he wanted to deal with this summer was his daughter's love life. "We leave for Yuma in an hour."

RACHEL STOOD IN HER father's foyer searching for the right words to break the tension. She settled on... "Your home is beautiful."

"I expect you don't remember living here."

"No, I don't," she said, refusing to lie. She motioned to the terra-cotta tile. "I like the floor."

"The kitchen's in the back." P.T. cut through a great room with an adobe fireplace and chunky furnishings—cowboy furniture. The kitchen was large and airy. A colorful mosaic-tile backsplash in deep gold, blue and red popped against the whitewashed walls. The cabinets were a dark distressed wood—the space above them held an array of brightly painted metal roosters. A wooden chopping block served as an island. P.T. caught Rachel studying the décor. "Anne—" he cleared his throat "—your mother had a rooster fetish."

"I like them." Rachel wondered if the bold, colorful fowl were indicative of her mother's personality.

"This was Anne's favorite room in the house."

The love in her father's voice when he spoke of her mother pierced Rachel's heart. Why couldn't he offer her a smidgen of that affection? She shifted under his scrutiny.

"You look like your mother," P.T. said.

Rachel had seen photos of Anne Lewis and agreed she was every inch her mother's daughter. "I could use a drink."

"Where are my manners?" Her father fetched a glass from the cupboard. "Lemonade or iced tea?"

A green-apple martini would have been better. "Iced tea." Rachel stared out the large picture window overlooking a courtyard. Trellises covered with red bougainvilleas had been mounted against the adobe wall and mounds of pink and yellow lantana grew in several planters. She couldn't picture the father she knew as someone who nurtured flowers. In the center of the patio sat a fountain with a bucking horse that spewed water from its mouth.

P.T. set Rachel's tea on the bistro table then leaned a hip against the butcher block. "That's Dust Devil." He pointed to the fountain. "He's the reason Five Star Ranch exists."

"How's that?"

"Anne caught Dust Devil being abused by a stock contractor." P.T. stared unseeingly across the room as if reliving the moment. "Your mother gave that cowboy a piece of her mind and threatened to call the authorities on him if he didn't hand over Dust Devil to her. Anne had a soft spot for abused animals, and she convinced me that it was my duty to provide a sanctuary for retired rough stock since I made a living off them." P.T. rubbed his chin. "Your mother was an astute woman, so I listened to her."

P.T. had loved Rachel's mother very much—what had happened to that man? "Was my mother happy living here?"

"Anne got lonely. There wasn't much for her to do until you came along." P.T.'s gaze slid away. "You were a precocious child."

"Aunt Edith talked about Mom often, but I was too young to remember any details about her." Rachel sipped her tea. "For some reason, though, when I smell the scent of roses I think of her."

A pained expression crossed her father's face. "Anne misted your bed sheets with rosewater before she tucked you in at night." P.T. cleared his throat then changed the subject. "You like working as a school psychologist? Teenagers can be a pain in the arse."

What did he know about teenage behaviors? He'd never visited Rachel during her high-school years. "I enjoy helping teens navigate difficult issues."

"Sounds as if you've found your calling."

Until this moment, Rachel had never expressed her appreciation to her father for paying her college tuition and graduate-school costs. She blamed her bad manners on the anger and resentment she harbored toward him. In light of P.T.'s recent cancer diagnosis, it was time to let a few things pass. "Thank you for paying off my student loans."

"The least I could do considering…"

Considering what? Had he been on the verge of apologizing for keeping his daughter at arm's length through the years? The air crackled with tension.

Rachel took pity on him. "Another thing I don't remember about my childhood is the heat."

"By the end of August even the natives have had enough of the sweltering temperatures." P.T. shook his head. "I'm sorry you had to come out here during the hottest part of the year."

"It's an adventure." One she hoped she wouldn't regret. "What have the doctors said about your condition?"

"Stage II prostate cancer."

"Which means?" Rachel knew nothing about prostate cancer except that stage I was better than stage II.

"The cancer hasn't spread outside the prostate, but if I don't get treatment soon, cancer cells could migrate to my lymph nodes."

"What kind of treatment plan has the doctor prescribed?"

"They're going to place a radioactive pellet in my prostate."

Ouch. "Why don't they take out your prostate?"

"Because of my age they believe this is the best way for now."

Her father was fifty-six. She guessed he was still sexually active...*don't go there.* "And the doctors are positive the cancer hasn't spread?"

"They'll do more tests once I check into the clinic in Phoenix."

Rachel worried about P.T. having to undergo a battery of procedures even though the tests were necessary for the doctors to determine the best course of treatment. "I could stay with you in Phoenix." As soon as the words left her mouth, she wanted to snatch them back. She hardly knew her father. Surely he wouldn't want her involved in his personal business.

"I'll be sitting on my duff doing nothing for weeks on end. I need you here." He glanced at his watch. "As a matter of fact, I asked my foreman to meet with me this afternoon. Let's head into my office and wait for him there."

After setting her glass in the sink, Rachel

trailed her father to the front of the house. They entered a room off the main foyer. Two leather chairs faced a massive desk littered with folders and loose papers. Was she expected to make heads or tails out of the mess? Before she asked the question the front door banged open.

"P.T., I can explain!" The frantic shout carried into the study.

Rachel pulled in a quick breath when she recognized the cowboy who burst into the room—the very same one whose blasted bull had dented the hood of her car.

No wonder her father had asked for her help this summer—if the ranch foreman couldn't keep a bull behind a fence, then he had no business running Five Star Rodeos.

Chapter Three

Clint stopped on a dime in the hallway outside P.T.'s office and stared at the woman who'd terrorized Curly.

Blue. Her eyes were a transparent blue like the Arizona sky on a cloudless day. The only sign she was surprised to see him was the subtle arch of a light-brown eyebrow.

Of all the rotten luck. How had the blonde tracked down Curly's home? She must have stopped in Stagecoach and asked questions. Shoot, every person within a hundred-mile radius of Five Star Ranch had butted heads with the bull on one occasion or another. Curly was a local legend.

"For God's sake, Clint." P.T. frowned. "What's got you riled?"

Clint wanted to shout "her." Instead, he said, "I can explain the dents in her—" *sissified* "—Prius."

"You hit my daughter's car?"

Daughter—as in the estranged *Rachel* P.T. rarely mentioned?

The woman whose sexy mouth he'd craved to taste a short while ago?

The woman who hadn't bothered to visit her father once since Clint had lived at the ranch? That Rachel?

Why had she shown up now? Had she heard about her father's cancer and felt guilty? Clint's gut insisted he shouldn't trust this woman. Caught up in staring at Rachel he remembered he hadn't answered P.T.'s question. "Curly dented the hood of her car."

"Blast it, Clint." P.T. motioned to the empty chair in front of the desk and Clint slid onto the leather seat. "You've got to keep that bull locked up. One of these days he'll roam onto the road and get someone killed." P.T. swung his gaze to Rachel. "You weren't injured, were you?"

"I'm fine."

"Clint will see to it that your car gets fixed."

Add auto repairs to the list of his duties this week. "I'm heading into Yuma later. I'll stop by Mel's place and make an appointment with the repair shop."

"No rush," P.T. said. "Rachel's staying all summer."

The bossy, no-sense-of-humor, sexy blonde was hanging around for three months?

You like her eyes.

True.

And she has great legs.

No argument there.

He wondered how long her hair was and if it was naturally blond or from a bottle.

"I plan to leave for Phoenix early in the morning," P.T. said.

"You'll be accompanying P.T. to Phoenix?" Clint spoke to Rachel.

"Actually—"

"I'm putting Rachel in charge of the rodeos this summer," P.T. said.

If he hadn't already been seated, Clint's legs would have buckled. He clenched the armrest until the skin over his knuckles threatened to split.

"Clint manages the rough-stock sanctuary but he's helped plenty with the rodeo-production schedule. If you have any questions, he's your go-to man," P.T. said.

Go-to man?

Don't lose your cool.

Not an easy task when P.T. had ripped Clint's guts out with his bare hands. Why had P.T. chosen his estranged daughter over Clint to manage the rodeos? Had he failed P.T. in some way and lost his trust?

P.T. was the first person in Clint's life who'd

made him feel as if he mattered as a human being. He'd worked side by side with P.T. for twenty-one years and Rachel had avoided visiting the ranch—yet, the first crisis the old man encountered, he'd turned to his daughter and not Clint.

"What do you do for a living?" Clint asked Rachel.

"I'm a high-school psychologist and athletic trainer."

Athletic trainer explained her toned, sleek legs but what the heck did a psychologist know about producing rodeos?

"My father assured me he has everything in order and all I need to do is make a few phone calls and follow up with vendors." Rachel's smile didn't reach her eyes.

The woman knew she was out of her league. What possible motivation did she have for taking on a job she was destined to fail?

Waving a leather notebook, P.T. said, "This is my rodeo bible. All the vendors' numbers are in here—contacts, dates and events. Keep track of the bottom line. We need to turn a profit this summer." P.T. left his chair and stood before the window. "Damned medical insurance only covers half my treatment."

"If you need money—"

Clint and Rachel stared at each other after

blurting the same words. If Rachel thought it odd that her father's employee offered financial assistance, she didn't say.

"I'm worried about the rough stock," P.T. said. "The money we make off the rodeos this summer has to buy enough feed and hay to get through next year."

P.T. rambled on about the rodeos but Clint didn't hear a word. He sat in a stupor, unable to comprehend how his longtime mentor, friend and the man he regarded as a father had chosen his estranged daughter to assume the helm of a company that had struggled the past few years to stay in the black.

"Although we got off on the wrong foot, I believe we'll be able to work together well." Rachel offered Clint her hand—firm and feminine, with neatly trimmed pink-painted nails. This woman did not belong on a ranch. "If you'll excuse me," she said, tugging her hand free. "I'll get my luggage."

"Clint will fetch your bags," P.T. said.

In less than ten minutes, Clint had gone from ranch foreman to mechanic to bellhop.

"I don't have much." Rachel left the room, leaving a trail of perfume-scented air in her wake.

Struggling to keep his mind from wandering outside with Rachel, Clint spoke to P.T.

"Haven't I proven I'm responsible enough to handle the rodeos?"

"Of course you can handle the rodeos."

"Then why would you ask your daughter to drive clear across the country to run a business she has no experience with?" He smoothed a hand over his close-cropped hair. "Rachel's a school shrink. Has she ever been to a rodeo before?"

"I'm not sure. You'll have to ask her."

"Is it because of Lauren? You're worried my daughter will be a distraction?"

"Not at all. Rachel's help will allow you to spend more time with Lauren."

"You're putting Rachel in charge to punish me because I haven't paid enough attention to Lauren over the years?"

"Hell, no!" P.T. banged his fist on the desk. "This isn't about you, Clint. It's about me. I want Rachel in charge of the rodeos. End of discussion."

"Whatever you say, boss."

P.T.'s head jerked as if Clint had slapped him. Add remorse to the crazy emotions running rampant inside Clint. P.T. had taken him in, given him a home and taught him to be a decent man. He deserved better from Clint.

"I'll make sure I'm available if Rachel needs me." Even if it killed him.

"Good. The doctors insist that if I beat this cancer and go into remission, I need to cut out the stress in my life."

"Are you talking retirement?" A sliver of excitement pricked Clint. He'd dreamed of one day running Five Star Rodeos.

"If Rachel does a good job this summer, I intend to ask her to stay on permanently."

Only sheer pride kept Clint from storming out of the room as his chest tightened, squeezing the air from his lungs. The hurt was like none he'd experienced. "Does Rachel—" he cleared his throat "—want to take over Five Star Rodeos?"

"I don't know. But she's my daughter. I owe her first right of refusal."

How did P.T. believe he *owed* Rachel his livelihood when she'd made no effort to be involved in his life? Clint lived at the ranch, took care of the animals and had been P.T.'s right-hand man for years.

On the heels of hurt came anger—mostly at himself for believing loyalty trumped genetics. Rachel was tied to P.T. by blood, not gratitude. Even though Clint believed he deserved to run the company, he was nothing but an adult foster kid—a castoff nobody had wanted.

"Are we finished talking?" Clint asked.

P.T. frowned, but Clint refused to apologize

for his curtness. Either way Clint viewed the situation, he was screwed. If Rachel failed then P.T. would assume Clint hadn't done enough to help her. If Rachel succeeded, she'd prove she was more than capable of managing the rodeo-production company.

"What's wrong, son?" P.T. asked.

Son? Right now Clint didn't feel much like P.T.'s son. Without another word, Clint left the office before he made promises he couldn't keep—like making sure nothing got in the way, including himself, of producing top-notch rodeos this summer.

As soon as Clint stepped outside the house, Rachel's spine stiffened. She didn't need a psychology degree to understand the handsome cowboy resented her presence. Why?

"Three bags?" Clint stopped next to the car and stared at the luggage.

Three suitcases was hardly a lot, considering she planned to stay the summer. "I'll bring in the rest," she said, referring to the tote bags containing her shoes, toiletries and miscellaneous items.

He hefted the luggage beneath his arms, the motion pulling his shirt taut against his broad shoulders. She forced her attention back to his face. "Clint."

"What?"

"You're angry."

The muscle along his jaw bulged and she expected him to storm off. He stayed.

"Are you upset that P.T.'s making you handle the repairs to my car?"

His brown eyes pierced her, stealing her breath. For an instant she imagined those eyes staring down at her as he... Shocked by her train of thought, she said, "We're going to be working together, which means we'll need to communicate." With words, not dark looks. Frustrated, she blurted, "Say something."

"P.T. believes you're the best person to produce his rodeos. I'll stay out of your way. You stay out of mine." He marched into the house with her luggage.

Was this the same cowboy who'd rescued Curly from the road? Unless... Had Clint expected to be put in charge of her father's business? Regardless, he didn't have to be rude.

"What'd you do to rile my dad?"

Rachel spun then slapped her palm against her thudding heart. Where had the pink-haired girl come from?

The teen smiled. "I get that kind of reaction a lot when people first see my hair."

"It's very...colorful."

Tugging a strand of shoulder-length hair,

the girl said, "It's the same color as Avril La-vigne's, only instead of highlights I colored my hair pink all over." She blew a bubble with her gum. "You know who Avril Lavigne is, don't you?"

"Sure, I've heard of the singer." Lots of girls in high school listened to the rock star's music. Rachel pointed toward the house. "Clint's your father?"

"Yeah, lucky me." She sighed. "I'm Lauren McGraw. Who are you?"

"Rachel Lewis from Rhode Island."

"I didn't know P.T. had a daughter. Cool."

Rachel's thoughts whizzed in all directions. "How old are you?"

"Eighteen. I'll be a senior in high school this fall."

"I don't recall seeing a high school when I drove through Stagecoach."

"There isn't one. I live in Los Angeles with my mom, but she's in Mexico with her new hus-band." Lauren blew another bubble then swal-lowed it whole inside her mouth. "I'm stuck here until my mom returns from her honey-moon in August." She didn't appear happy with the situation.

"You said you'll be a senior this fall. Are you excited about graduating?"

"I guess. First, I have to pass two killer courses, AP biology and precalculus."

The difficult classes confirmed a good brain beneath all the pink hair. Since the girl appeared willing to chat—unlike her father—Rachel said, "I work at a high school."

"What subject do you teach?"

"I'm not a teacher. I'm a school psychologist."

"Whoa!" Lauren raised her hands in the air and backed up a step. "Did my dad ask you to come here?"

Caught off guard by the outburst Rachel asked, "What do you mean?"

"He thinks because I dyed my hair pink and pierced my eyebrow and nose that I'm going to join a gang or start doing drugs. That's why you're here, isn't it? To—" Lauren made quote signs in the air "—straighten me out."

"I'm not here to straighten anyone out. P.T. asked me to help with his rodeos while he's in Phoenix."

Rachel's statement knocked the wind out of Lauren's sails. "Really? 'Cause I wouldn't put it past my dad to—"

"Put what past me?" Clint asked.

Lauren pointed at Rachel. "She's a shrink."

"So?"

"I'm not letting her inside my head no matter what you or she thinks about my hair color."

"I don't mind the pink." Rachel ignored Clint's shocked stare. "I'm all in favor of individuality." Most teens experimented with different identities until they found where they fit in best.

"I might add neon-green highlights before school starts. Avril did that once and she looked—"

"Enough talk about hair. Are you ready to head into Yuma?" Clint asked Lauren.

"Do you want to come, Rachel? Yuma's a decent-size town with name-brand stores. There's a Starbucks—"

"I doubt—"

"I'd love to go." Rachel cut off Clint's objection. *Love* was stretching it, but she was determined to show Clint that she didn't intimidate easily.

"Might as well follow in your car," Clint said. "We'll drop it off at the repair shop."

"Sounds like a plan." Rachel faced angry teenagers on a daily basis, so handling a good-looking, disgruntled cowboy should be a piece of cake.

Or not.

"*She* gets my hair," Lauren said to Clint as they waited in his truck outside Mel's Auto Repair in Yuma.

Rachel had been discussing repairs with Mel for the past fifteen minutes. "*Her* opinion doesn't count." His gaze shifted to the side mirror on the driver's door. As far as women went, Rachel was damn easy on the eyes, but too... Several adjectives came to mind—opinionated, self-assured, serious, uppity and educated.

"What do you have against Rachel?"

"Nothing," Clint protested.

Lauren sipped her designer coffee. "I think she's okay."

What was taking Rachel so long? She probably believed Mel was trying to rip her off. The shop owner was a fair man and had worked on Clint's truck twice—after the front fender had collided with a boulder and the back fender with a water tank. Rachel wouldn't find a better deal anywhere. "Wait here." He strode across the parking lot and entered the business.

"I refuse to leave my car without a written estimate." Rachel pursed her mouth, the seductive pout drawing Clint's gaze to her lips. He really wanted to discover for himself if the pink gloss tasted like cotton candy or bubble gum.

The mechanic sent Clint a pleading look. "Mel does the best work in the area. His prices are fair and he doesn't overcharge for labor or parts."

"That's fine but I'm not letting him touch the Prius without a written estimate."

"I'm swamped today, but I'll contact Toyota tomorrow and find out how long it will take to order the paint," Mel said. "Those sissy colors are hard to come by."

Rachel glared. "He won't stop mocking my car."

Clint pressed his lips together to keep from chuckling.

"I want a second opinion on repairing the Prius." Rachel stormed out the door. If she didn't trust Clint's advice about car repairs, he doubted she'd accept his suggestions on running P.T.'s rodeos.

"Whoo-wee. The little lady's hell on wheels."

"That's Rachel Lewis, P.T.'s daughter."

"Didn't know P.T. had a daughter." Mel shook his head. "I don't mind working on her car. I could use the money."

"She won't find a better deal than your garage. We'll be back." An hour later, Clint parked the truck at Mel's Auto Repair and Rachel pulled the Prius into a spot next to his truck and headed for the mechanic's office.

Lauren groaned. "Oh, my God. Is Rachel ever going to make up her mind?"

"We'll see." Even though he'd vouched for Mel's work, he admired Rachel's thoroughness in comparing prices—wasteful spending drove him nuts.

Clint's stomach growled. Lunch had been seven hours ago. "Where do you want to eat?"

"Chili's. I like their Cajun pasta."

"Maybe we should ask Rachel, since she's a guest." More guest than family, in his opinion. A few minutes later Rachel opened the passenger-side door and hopped into the truck.

"Any problems?" he asked.

"Mel's charging an extra ten dollars."

"What for?" Clint asked.

"He tacked on a nuisance fee."

Clint stared and Lauren giggled.

"Laugh all you want but for the extra ten bucks I got a written estimate." Rachel waved the piece of paper in the air.

"We're going to Chili's for supper. Is that okay with you?" Lauren asked.

"Sure. They've got decent salads," Rachel said. "I try to avoid eating too much red meat."

Go figure. P.T.'s daughter was a health nut. A half hour later, Rachel changed Clint's mind when she ordered a salad with chicken meat and devoured her share of chips and salsa.

"More chips?" the waitress asked, stopping at their table.

"Sure." Lauren handed over the empty basket.

"Don't eat too many chips or you won't finish your supper," Clint said.

Lauren made a tsking sound. "I think I'm old enough to monitor my food intake."

"Then you'd better finish your meal, since I'm paying for it."

"If you're going to make a big deal out of a few chips, I'll pay for my supper." Lauren tossed her napkin on the table and said, "Move. I have to use the bathroom."

Clint slipped from the booth then exhaled loudly after his daughter walked off.

"You shouldn't do that," Rachel said.

"Do what?"

"Let your daughter disrespect you."

Clint's hackles rose. "Do you have children?"

"No."

"Then you shouldn't be doling out advice."

"I work with angsty teenagers. You have to stand your ground and demand their respect or they'll walk all over you."

He opened his mouth to tell Rachel to mind her own business but was cut short when Lauren returned to the table. With half an ear he listened to the females chat, fuming over Rachel sticking her nose into his and Lauren's business.

The check arrived and he insisted on paying for Rachel's meal, even though she protested. When they hit the outskirts of Yuma, Lauren put in her earbuds and listened to music on her iPod. Clint focused on the road, ignoring Rachel's stare. Ignoring the clean, fresh scent of her perfume was more difficult. It had been forever since he'd sat next to a nice-smelling female. Assuming she had more parenting suggestions to offer him, he said, "Spit it out."

"Spit what out?"

"Whatever's bugging you?" When she remained quiet, he said, "You've been staring at me since we left the restaurant."

"We need to clear the air between us."

"I didn't know it was polluted."

"Funny. I'm being serious."

What was it with females—always overanalyzing or making a big deal out of nothing?

"You're not comfortable with me running P.T.'s rodeo company."

He should have known a woman with a psychology major would find a way inside his head. "P.T. has his reasons for choosing you."

"But you don't like me."

He liked plenty about her physical appearance.

"There's annoyance in your eyes when you look at me," she said.

Really? Rachel must not have had much experience with men if she misinterpreted his appreciative glances as irritation. "I apologize for being rude."

"I wasn't asking for an apology."

Jeez. Following the woman's train of thought was like trailing Curly into the desert—he never knew which direction the bull might mosey. Honesty was the best course of action. "You want to clear the air? How about this—P.T. made a mistake handing over the reins to you."

She stiffened. "You know nothing about me."

Exactly. "Have you ever been to a rodeo?"

"No."

"I rest my case," he said.

"Just because I've never seen cowboys ride bucking stock doesn't mean I lack business sense."

"Do you have experience putting on large events?"

"I organized a fundraiser for the weight room at the high school. We collected four thousand dollars for new equipment."

"You got any idea how much money is involved in producing a Five Star Rodeo?"

"No."

"The average cost runs between a hundred-fifty and two hundred thousand dollars."

Rachel's face paled.

"Like P.T. stated earlier, the rodeos have to

turn a profit or there won't be enough money to support the sanctuary ranch the following year."

"My father never mentioned his business was struggling."

"Things are tight, leaving little room for mistakes. That's not to say there isn't more competition in the rodeo business these days, because there is. Some of the production companies are using expensive gimmicks to increase attendance."

"What kinds of gimmicks?"

"Drawings for free vehicles. Time-shares in the Bahamas."

"Can you recommend a dealership that might be willing to donate a truck to one of our rodeos?" she asked.

He could but why should he help Rachel look good in P.T.'s eyes? "Sorry, I don't have any connections to car salesmen."

"There has to be a way to increase attendance without breaking the bank," she said.

"Guess you'll figure something out. That's why P.T. put you in charge, right?"

Chapter Four

6:00 a.m. Monday morning Clint stood next to P.T.'s truck speculating whether or not Rachel would haul her backside out of bed and wish her father good luck with his cancer treatments.

"Maybe her alarm clock didn't go off." Clint took one step toward the house before P.T. snagged his arm.

"Leave her be, son."

"She's your daughter." Clint ground his back teeth together.

P.T.'s shoulders sagged.

In the ten minutes they'd hee-hawed with goodbyes, P.T. had aged before Clint's eyes. "Lauren's wanted to shop at the outlets in Phoenix. We'll drive you up there, check you in at the medical center, then we—"

"No." P.T. stared at the front door. "Rachel needs you here."

If your daughter needs my help, why did you ask her to run the business? Had P.T. considered what might become of his deceased wife's dream if the rodeos failed? If there wasn't enough money to feed the livestock next year, the animals would end up at the glue factory.

"Are you sure you want Rachel to manage the rodeos?" Clint asked.

"You don't believe she can handle the responsibility."

That's right.

"Never underestimate my daughter. She inherited my bullheadedness."

Inherit... The word reminded Clint that he was an employee, not a family member. "Is that why she didn't get out of bed to say goodbye to you?"

"There are two sides to every story and often neither one is right." P.T. climbed into his truck, started the engine then lowered the driver-side window. "I'll phone after I'm settled in."

"Let us know what day of the week would be good to visit."

P.T. shook his head. "You and Rachel will be too busy with the rodeos."

"Lauren won't stand for not seeing you all summer."

The mention of Clint's daughter made P.T. smile. Clint swore P.T. had yet to crack a smile when he spoke of Rachel.

"You keep that youngun' busy so she stays out of trouble."

Lauren had balked at spending the summer in Stagecoach, but as soon as she'd arrived she'd taken to P.T. The old man doted on her like an adoring grandfather. He had patience with the cranky teenager and Lauren made P.T. laugh with her outrageous comments on ranch life.

"Make sure she reads the Zane Grey novels I left on my desk. I told her I'd read that sci-fi romance she never stops talking about." P.T. lifted his eReader off the front seat. "Got the book downloaded right here."

The old man wasn't afraid of technology. P.T. had the most up-to-date software programs installed on his computer and this past Christmas, Clint had given him a GPS gadget for his golf game. The salesclerk at the store had attempted to explain how the device worked, but gave up after Clint asked too many questions. When P.T. had opened his gift he'd figured out how to use it in less than five minutes.

Even though P.T. kept the company's financial statements and records on the computer, old habits die hard. The boss spent hours writing duplicate information into a ledger. As much as he embraced technology, P.T. didn't trust what he couldn't see or hold in his hands.

"I'm sure Lauren will call you to discuss the books."

"Don't pester the girl. We'll talk when I return in August."

For some reason P.T. was determined to undergo his treatment without family support. Stubborn man. "Drive safe and…" What the hell did you say to a man who stared his own mortality in the face? "Stay well."

"Will do."

Clint didn't know how long he stood in the yard watching the taillights of P.T.'s truck when the front door burst open and Rachel rushed outside. Wearing sandals, a skimpy pair of shorts, a tank top and her blond hair snarled, she appeared frantic. Then she saw Clint and trotted toward him, her small, braless breasts jiggling beneath the shirt. He couldn't remember any of his high-school teachers looking as hot as Rachel. The closer she came, the faster his pulse raced. Her fresh-from-bed rumpled appearance sent his libido into overdrive. *Steady, man.* Finding himself sexually attracted to a pretty woman wasn't unusual—as long as he didn't allow that attraction to evolve into something deeper.

"Where's P.T.?" she asked, stopping a few feet away.

"He already left." Clint pointed to the dust in the air a mile down the road.

"For Phoenix?"

"Yep. Nice of you to get out of bed and wish him well." Rachel gasped but Clint refused to feel remorse for his biting comment. What kind of daughter didn't care enough to say good-bye to her father? He and Lauren hadn't always been on the best of terms but he believed she'd stand by his side in the face of adversity.

"He did that on purpose." Rachel's eyelashes fluttered. Was she blinking back tears?

"Did what?" Clint crossed his arms over his chest, determined to resist the sudden urge to hug Rachel.

"He left before I got out of bed."

"P.T. couldn't wait forever."

"Last night he said he'd leave at eight o'clock. I offered to cook him breakfast."

Clint checked his watch. 6:46 a.m.

"P.T. left early because I insisted on going with him today," she said.

Certain she was all talk and no action, Clint pulled a set of keys from his pocket. "Feel free to use the truck in the barn."

She snatched the key ring from his fingers and dashed off, leaving him gaping. A moment later she put the pedal to the metal and zipped past Clint.

"I'll be damned. She does care."

What the heck was Rachel going to do if she caught P.T.—escort him to Phoenix in her pj's? He'd made it to the porch of the cabin when he spotted her heading back to the ranch. She parked near the barn.

"Well?" Clint said the moment Rachel opened the driver-side door.

"He doesn't want company." Her indifferent shrug was at odds with the pinched expression on her face.

Feeling compelled to offer a token of sympathy Clint said, "I insisted on going, too, but he's a prideful man."

"Will he be okay driving by himself?"

The note of concern in her voice bothered Clint. Had he misjudged her relationship with P.T.? *There are two sides...* A mad dash down the road wasn't proof she cared about a man she'd ignored all her life. "P.T. will be fine. He promised to call once he checked into the clinic."

"You'll let me know when you hear from him," Rachel said.

"Sure. I'll be in the barn most of the morning if you run into trouble."

"Thanks, but I don't foresee encountering any problems." Head held high, she walked off.

Clint stared at her firm fanny, unsure what

to make of P.T.'s daughter. When the front door shut, he did an about-face and retreated to the barn, fearing this would be a hotter-than-normal summer if he didn't rein in his attraction to Rachel.

Two hours later Rachel entered the barn and announced, "We've got a problem."

Clint set aside the pitchfork and studied her. She'd changed into khaki shorts and a green T-shirt. And a bra. He preferred her without one. Forcing his gaze from her sexy legs he focused on her face. Blue eyes clouded with worry and her teeth nibbled her lower lip, drawing his attention to her very kissable mouth.

"What do you mean, *we* have a problem?" he asked.

"The rodeo secretary called and—"

"Barb Hamilton?"

"She retired as of today."

"You're joking?"

"No, I'm not."

Losing a rodeo secretary two weeks before the first event was a disaster. Barb would never leave P.T. hanging without a good reason. "Is she ill?"

"Barb's fine. Her daughter had a baby recently but suffered complications."

"Is her daughter okay?"

"She will be, but Barb needs to help care for the baby while her daughter recovers."

What else could go wrong the first day P.T. was gone?

"I could assume the secretary's duties and save my father money."

Was it false bravado or stupidity that prompted Rachel to volunteer for a position she had no experience with? He closed the space between them, stopping short when he caught a whiff of perfume-scented air. "Do you know what a secretary does?"

"I'm guessing she keeps track of the expenditures for each rodeo?"

Not even close. "Barb is in charge of processing entry fees, checking in the contestants when they arrive for the rodeo. She calculates the winners and cuts the checks for the cowboys and she creates the score sheets used that day by the officials. Then she gathers the sheets after each event and posts the standings. She also keeps track of the cowboy and livestock matchups, then informs the cowboys when they call in wanting to know which animal they're scheduled to ride, as well as what score or time they need in order to place."

"I expect this Barb of all wonders also deals with the media?"

"The press phoned?"

"The *Canyon City Courier* wants to run a story on the upcoming rodeo."

"You didn't tell them that P.T.'s in Phoenix undergoing cancer treatments, did you?"

"Of course not. I wouldn't want people believing my father's health might interfere with producing a successful rodeo."

Score a point for Rachel—the woman might not know a damned thing about the sport of rodeo but she possessed common sense. "Barb will be tough to replace," he said. "She's a four-time National Finals Rodeo secretary. Her mother was inducted into the Pro Rodeo Hall of Fame for her career as a rodeo secretary."

"Is that your way of saying I can't handle the job?" Rachel asked.

"Take my word for it, you can't. Did you ask Barb to recommend a replacement?"

"She offered the name of a woman who might be willing to cover for her. When I phoned the lady and introduced myself as P.T.'s daughter, she said P.T. didn't have a daughter and I should be ashamed of making prank calls. Then she hung up on me."

"You didn't tell her—"

"How exactly does one explain their father kept their existence a secret?"

Obviously Rachel was hurt that P.T. hadn't

told people about her, but what did she expect when she hadn't acted like a true daughter?

"I don't have time to make any calls until later." Rachel had a lot to learn if she believed every time she encountered a roadblock he'd drop what he was doing and handle the situation.

"Her name's Nancy. Don't wait too long to contact her. If she can't fill in for Barb, we need time to find someone else ASAP." Rachel stomped out of the barn, her tight little fanny twitching right, left and right.

The stirring inside Clint's jeans reminded him that his last roll in the hay had been over nine months ago—right before his on-again-off-again girlfriend, Monica, had ditched him for a Vegas gambler who'd promised her diamond rings and fancy dinners at five-star hotels.

Damn. Why did he have to be attracted to Rachel when her very presence threatened his relationship with P.T.?

RACHEL ENTERED HER father's house and slammed the door behind her. She couldn't believe she'd been on the job less than twenty-four hours and already had a major crisis on her hands—one she was ill prepared to handle, as Clint had kindly pointed out. *The schmuck.*

"What's wrong?" Lauren stepped into the

hallway, the black cat from the yard snuggled in her arms.

"Nothing," Rachel lied. She motioned to the feline. "Who's your friend?"

"Felix. I promised P.T. I'd feed him while he was gone." Lauren set Felix on the floor and he scurried off. "What are you doing today?"

"Making phone calls." Rachel entered P.T.'s office.

Lauren followed Rachel into the office. "I'm bored."

"Your father could probably use your help with ranch chores."

"My dad's so lame. No way am I helping him clean horse stalls."

"You shouldn't disrespect your father."

"What do you mean?" Lauren's brow puckered.

"You called him lame. That's rude."

"Yeah, well, using me as free labor all summer is rude, too."

Clint had his hands full with the teen. Rachel shuffled through a stack of papers on the desk, searching for a phone number she'd scribbled down earlier.

"You're miffed," Lauren said.

"I received some unsettling news this morning."

Lauren's eyes widened. "It's not about P.T., is it?"

"No. P.T.'s fine." She glanced at the wall clock. "He's probably in Phoenix by now."

"I like P.T. He's cool and he doesn't care if my hair's pink." Lauren's gaze landed on the books piled on the corner of the desk. "His Zane Grey novels." She grabbed the first book. "I guess you figured out this is your dad's favorite author."

Rachel hadn't known her father loved the famous writer of Westerns.

"P.T. made a bet with me," Lauren said. "He promised to read *Planet Destiny* if I read one of his Zane Grey novels. We're both trying to broaden our horizons." Lauren smiled. "I wonder what he'll think of the outer-space romance."

"I thought the author did a great job building a believable science-fiction world," Rachel said. She'd read *Planet Destiny* because half the girls in the school were fans of the alien love story. In order for Rachel to better help her students she had to understand what they were interested in and where they were coming from.

"I hated that Zordan died at the end, but I bet the author will write a sequel and bring him back to life." Lauren scooped the rest of the books from the desk. "What's the bad news you got this morning?"

Rachel didn't want to burden the teen but there was no one else to talk to. "The rodeo secretary quit and I need to find a replacement before the Canyon City event a week from next Saturday."

"Ask my dad. He'll know who to call."

"I did. He's going to contact a woman for me."

"That's good, right?"

"Only if the woman agrees to help us out." Lauren appeared in no hurry to leave. Wanting to appease her curiosity about Clint's relationship with her father, Rachel asked, "How long has your dad worked at the ranch?"

"Since he was a kid."

A kid? Wait a minute. "So your grandparents lived and worked on the ranch?"

"I don't think my dad knows who his parents are. He doesn't share a lot of his childhood with me, because it wasn't very good," Lauren said. "But then, what kid has a perfect childhood?"

Amen to that.

"Dad was a foster child but ran away at sixteen. P.T. took him in and he's never left the ranch."

"How old is your father?"

"Thirty-seven."

Shock squeezed the oxygen from Rachel's lungs. She'd have been seven or eight when Clint arrived at the ranch. Aunt Edith must have known about the situation—had she kept the knowledge to herself because she feared the news would hurt Rachel? And hurt it did. How could her own father have sent her away then a few years later take in a sixteen-year-old boy?

"Don't you feel well?" Lauren's gaze dropped to Rachel's hand pressed against her stomach.

"Indigestion from breakfast," Rachel mumbled. She'd answered her father's call for help because she'd desired to reconnect with him. To repair the damage he'd inflicted when he'd emotionally abandoned her. Damned if P.T. wasn't testing her good intentions. The realization that Clint had more of a right to call Five Star Ranch home than she did squeezed her heart like a vise.

"Lauren, if you'll excuse me I need to make a few calls."

"Oh, yeah, sure." The teen left the office and a moment later the sound of the front door closing echoed in the foyer.

Refusing to cry, Rachel sank into the desk chair and closed her eyes. No wonder Clint hadn't been thrilled when her father had put her in charge of his rodeo company. After liv-

ing with him for years, Clint was protective of
P.T.—a man he'd come to view as a father.

Well, tough. P.T. was *her* father—not Clint's.

Rachel's mind raced through the years,
searching for clues her aunt might have given
that P.T. had been raising a teenager, but nothing stood out in her memory. Lauren said Clint
had run from foster care. Rachel guessed there
was some consolation in knowing Clint hadn't
been the result of her father having had an af-
fair. P.T. may consider Clint his son, but Rachel
held one advantage over the ranch hand—she
was P.T.'s daughter by blood.

This was her one chance to show her father
that she, not the kid P.T. had taken in off the
streets, deserved recognition. Rachel would
do everything in her power to make sure the
summer rodeos succeeded—beyond her father's
wildest imagination.

What happens after you make your point?

The pent-up anger inside Rachel escaped in
a harsh wheeze. She didn't know what she expected from her father—an apology? *Yes.* Rachel needed P.T. to admit he regretted sending
her to live with his sister.

I'm sorry wouldn't erase his mistake, but at
least admitting regret would clear the way for
them to establish a new relationship.

"What did Nancy say?"

Startled, Clint glanced up from behind P.T.'s desk. Rachel hovered in the doorway. Had she eavesdropped on his call to the secretary? "Nancy will cover the rodeo on the twentieth and the following two if we like her work."

"Is she asking for the same pay as Barb?"

"No. Nancy wants two hundred dollars more per rodeo."

Rachel stepped farther into the room and shut the door. "You didn't think to ask me if that was okay?"

"I didn't ask you because it wouldn't have mattered whether you'd agreed to her fee or not. Nancy refused to work for less."

"You didn't even try to negotiate with her."

Rachel's statement proved she'd listened in on the call. Clearly she didn't trust him. No matter, he didn't trust her, either. Clint could have sweet-talked Nancy into taking less pay, but he had no burning desire to make things easier on Rachel.

"P.T. set a firm budget per rodeo."

"If you can do better, contact Nancy and re-negotiate her pay." He held out the cordless phone and he and Rachel engaged in a stare down. She glanced away first.

"I'm heading out to check on the water

tanks—" Clint rounded the desk "—in case another crisis arises that you can't handle."

"Don't worry. I won't inconvenience you again."

Clint couldn't leave the house fast enough—frustration and guilt nipping at his boot heels. Paying the rodeo secretary a few extra bucks wasn't a big deal. Besides, Rachel screwing up and falling short in P.T.'s eyes might be the only way Clint could keep a toehold in the family. Damn it, P.T. was like a father to Clint and he refused to step aside willingly.

"Hey, Dad." Lauren's voice stopped Clint before he reached the end of the walking path. "Where are you going?"

"To check the water tanks. Why don't you come with me?"

"And do what? Watch animals drink?" Lauren moved closer. "Can we go somewhere?"

Smack-dab in the middle of the day? Clint considered the chores waiting for him when he returned from checking the water supply. "I'm busy 'til supper time."

"You're always busy." Lauren stamped her foot. "What about me? I'm stuck here with nothing to do."

"You could read the books P.T. left for you."

"Like I'm supposed to read until dinner? That's five hours from now."

Not wanting to argue with his daughter, Clint fished his wallet from his back pocket and handed her fifty dollars. "Take the ranch truck into town and get your nails done."

His suggestion erased the scowl from her face.

"If you want, we'll watch the movie that came in the mail on Saturday." Once he discovered Lauren was a night owl, staying up until one or two in the morning, he'd signed up for Netflix so she could watch movies in her bedroom after he hit the sack following the nightly news.

"It's another zombie picture," she said.

Great. Lauren was into vampires, zombies and werewolves—not Clint's cup of tea but he'd gladly lose a few hours of sleep tonight if it pacified his daughter and allowed him to get his work done. "Guess I'll be a zombie expert by the end of the summer."

"Cool." Lauren retreated to the cabin.

"Do you always do that?" Rachel stood near the paloverde tree by the front door. Did she intend to trail him around the ranch and spy on him?

"Do I always do what?" Clint asked.

"Give in to your daughter if she whines loud and long enough."

"My relationship with Lauren isn't any of your business."

"True, but if you haven't already figured it out, teens will try to manipulate the adults in their world at every turn."

"Lauren isn't manipulating me."

"Yes, she is. She's figured out that if she complains loud and long enough she'll either get her way or get your money."

Damn Rachel. Wasn't it enough that she was running the show for P.T.? Did she have to point out Clint's failings as a father, too? "Did you want something or did you just step outside to give me parenting advice?"

"I forgot to ask if you'd heard anything from P.T. I called his cell phone three times today but he's not picking up."

"P.T. doesn't like to talk on the phone." Rachel would have known that if she'd attempted to contact her father through the years.

"If he calls, will you let me know?"

"Sure. Anything else?"

"No."

Clint made a beeline for his truck and sped away, ticked off at Rachel—not so much because she poked her nose into his relationship with Lauren, but because she'd been right. In order to keep the peace, Clint was allowing Lauren to walk all over him. Regardless, how he handled his daughter was his business, not Rachel's. He and Lauren were still finding their way as father and daughter. Eventually things would settle down between them and he'd no longer feel pressured to cave in to her demands.

Chapter Five

By Friday afternoon Rachel's nerves were frayed. The simple task of contacting the rodeo sponsors had taken more time than she'd anticipated because representatives from the companies wouldn't return her calls. She'd been forced to change tactics and drop by their places of business to meet in person, but that proved worthless as the business owners wanted to know why P.T. wasn't the one securing their financial pledges. She'd hemmed and hawed, which had only increased their suspicion of her.

Rachel had considered asking Clint to intervene on her behalf, but she hadn't wanted to admit defeat and doubted he'd help her after she'd overstepped her bounds and criticized his parenting skills. *Good grief.* What had gotten into her—telling the foreman how to raise his daughter?

After speaking with the sponsors, Rachel had checked in with the program announcer. Jim

Fendwick had pestered Rachel, demanding to know why she and not P.T. had phoned to discuss the particulars of each rodeo. Rachel had fast-talked her way past the subject, promising that P.T. would touch base with Jim soon. Next on her to-do list was phoning the stock contractor and verifying the animals' arrival twenty-four hours prior to the rodeos—the first of which took place in Canyon City, Saturday, June twentieth—eight days from now.

"Hey, Rachel?" Lauren waltzed into the office.

Another interruption. "What can I do for you?" Rachel sifted through the yellow sticky notes she'd compiled during the week, searching for the stock contractor's number.

"I forgot to tell you someone called the foreman's cabin this morning after Dad left to check the animals."

"Who was it?"

"Mitch O'Donnell or McDonnell…or Mc—"

"McDonnell." The mayor of Canyon City. Why had he called Clint and not her? She'd made it clear the last time she spoke with the mayor that she and not Clint was in charge of the Canyon City Rodeo. How was she to get anything done if no one trusted her? "What did Mr. McDonnell want?"

"He asked why P.T. wasn't answering his cell phone."

"Did you tell him I'd return his call?"

"Yeah, but he sounded ticked off."

"I'm sorry he was rude to you."

"That's okay. Once I told him P.T. was in Phoenix getting cancer treatments he got all worried and apologized."

Rachel's stomach plummeted. Hadn't Clint elicited a promise from his daughter to keep P.T.'s medical condition a secret? "Lauren, if people ask about P.T., please don't tell them he has cancer or where he is."

The teen's eyes widened. "Did I do something wrong?"

"P.T.'s a private person—" at least when it came to telling his friends and business associates he had a daughter "—and he doesn't want people discussing his health or worrying the rodeos won't be up to Five Star standards without him at the helm."

"But my dad will make sure they are."

If no one had faith in Rachel, why had P.T. picked her as his replacement? Swallowing her anger, she said, "Promise you won't mention P.T.'s medical condition to anyone."

"Okay, sure." Lauren backpedaled out of the room and shut the door.

Rachel practiced her yoga breathing—long,

deep breaths to help calm her body and focus her mind. One mistake shouldn't hurt. Hopefully Mayor McDonnell wouldn't spread rumors about P.T.'s health. Feeling less panicky, Rachel spent the next few hours tracking down the stock contractor.

At three o'clock in the afternoon the mayor of Canyon City phoned and Rachel knew she was in big trouble. "Mr. McDonnell, please calm down. I'll answer all your questions."

"Is it true P.T. has cancer?"

"Yes, but let me assure you he's going to be fine." After Lauren had let the cat out of the bag there wasn't much Rachel could do but attempt to smother the fire.

"P.T.'s in Phoenix?"

"He's undergoing treatments prescribed by his doctor. He'll be returning to Stagecoach some time in August."

"Why didn't P.T. put Clint McGraw in charge?"

"Clint's busy with the rough-stock sanctuary."

"And who are you?"

"P.T.'s daughter, Rachel."

"Didn't know he had a daughter."

You and everyone else. "I'm staying at Five Star Ranch the entire summer, making sure the rodeos proceed as scheduled. I have everything under—"

"What do you know about running a rodeo?"

She couldn't very well tell the mayor she was flying by the seat of her pants. "Mr. McDonnell, P.T. left detailed instructions—"

"We're going to have to cancel the rodeo."

Rachel's heart stalled.

The mayor argued that news of P.T.'s cancer would spread through the rodeo community and he couldn't take any chances on low attendance numbers.

"Why would P.T.'s cancer affect attendance?" she asked.

"Canyon City is a small town and the rodeo is our biggest moneymaker of the year. Most businesses earn the bulk of their yearly income during that weekend."

"How does this relate to ticket sales?"

"Once the top contenders hear P.T. isn't running the show, they'll worry about getting paid and pull out for more sure bets elsewhere. If the big names aren't competing in the rodeo, folks won't waste their money on a ticket."

"But—"

"I got elected mayor because I promised the people of Canyon City that I'd do everything possible to bring more commerce to the town. Besides, I have to think about my reelection next year. I'm better off booking a traveling carnival than taking a chance on Five Star Rodeos."

"I've spoken to the sponsors and they're committed to following through with their financial pledges."

"Saying and doing are two different things."

The mayor refused to budge an inch.

"I'll devise a public-relations campaign that promises to meet or exceed last year's attendance numbers. If the sponsors see a jump in advance ticket sales they're not going to back out, and the top contenders won't cancel, either." If only Rachel was as confident in her plan as she sounded.

"We're running out of time, young lady."

"Give me until Monday to present a plan to you and your council members. If you still don't believe the rodeo will be successful then you're free to cancel the event."

A loud sigh filled Rachel's ear. "You've got until Monday to restore my faith in Five Star Rodeos."

"What were last year's ticket sales, Mr. McDonnell?"

"Twenty-two thousand."

Reasonable. "What's the population of Canyon City?"

"Two thousand seventy-three."

Oh. My. God.

"I'll gather the council members together and we'll meet you at Fran's Waffle House off the interstate at three o'clock Monday."

"Fran's Waffle House. Got it. Thank you, Mr. McDonnell."

"Don't thank me yet, young lady."

Rachel disconnected the call and the phone rang immediately. The Mayor of Boot Hill, Arizona, was calling to cancel the rodeo. Rachel explained the situation and the mayor agreed to meet at the waffle house to hear her plan. Rachel didn't give the mayor of Piney Gorge a chance to phone her—she extended an invite to the waffle-house meeting and the mayor agreed to attend.

Once Rachel had spoken to all three mayors, she vomited in the wastebasket beneath the desk. Carrying the trash can, she staggered from the office, stopping once to toss her cookies in the hallway. After retreating to the bathroom and cleaning out the can, Rachel sank to the floor and battled tears.

Why was it so damned important that she not disappoint her father when he'd let her down all her life? And darn it. Why had P.T. given her a job she wasn't qualified to do?

She should pack her bags, hand over the rodeo bible to Clint and return to Rhode Island where she was appreciated and missed by her friends and coworkers.

Clint would love that. Too bad for the cowboy, she wasn't a quitter.

Rachel brushed her teeth and gargled with mouthwash. Feeling better and less anxious she went in search of Clint only to learn from Lauren that he'd gone to check on the livestock. Too impatient to wait for him to return, she grabbed her sunglasses and the extra set of keys for the old truck in the barn, then followed the road Lauren said Clint had taken.

Five miles later the trail ended at the base of a rocky incline. Rachel hiked the small hill to gain a better view of the area, regretting that she hadn't exchanged her sandals for athletic shoes when thorny weeds brushed her ankles and tiny pebbles lodged between her toes. Gaze glued to the ground she prayed a snake wouldn't slither out from beneath a rock and strike her. As soon as she reached the summit she located Clint's truck in the distance.

Although she remained upset, she took a moment to appreciate the scenery—a shirtless cowboy working under the blazing Arizona sun against the backdrop of the Bryan Mountains and a desert terrain dotted with cacti. The view was breathtaking—the cowboy even more so. She watched Clint use a shovel to move large rocks away from the ground in front of the water tank, the muscles in his back and arms bunching and rippling. If his upper body was this impressive she could only imagine what the rest of him looked like.

Knock it off and quit ogling a half-naked man.

Rachel shouted Clint's name and waved her hat in the air, but she went unnoticed as he continued to clear a path around the steel stock tank. Five minutes passed and Rachel's arms began to burn from the sun. She doubted the sunscreen she'd applied after breakfast would do any good this late in the day.

Clint set the shovel in the truck bed, then pulled the hose from the stock tank and turned toward the hill. Rachel stuck her fingers between her lips and let out a shrill whistle, which caught his attention. He signaled her to wait for him, then hopped into his truck and drove along a path that skirted the hill.

"What's wrong?" he shouted as soon as he shifted into Park. "Is Lauren hurt?"

"No, she's fine." Rachel barely got the words out as she became mesmerized by the bead of sweat rolling down the center of his tanned chest. The shimmering ball of liquid headed straight for the dark patch of hair peeking above the damp waistband of his jeans.

"What are you doing out here?" he asked, shifting his stance, the movement drawing the water pellet closer to his belly button.

Suddenly Rachel became dizzy. "I think I need to sit down."

Swearing beneath his breath Clint leaned inside the truck, started the engine and shoved her onto the front seat where he directed an air-conditioning vent at her face. Before she had a chance to speak he handed her a water bottle from the cooler in the back.

She guzzled the liquid then gasped. "Nobody believes I can run Five Star Rodeos." She waved a hand in the air. "They haven't even met me but they've judged me and found me lacking."

"Who's judged you?"

"Mayor McDonnell. Barbara, the supersecretary. Her replacement, Nancy what's-her-name—"

"Nancy Smith."

"Jim Fendwick."

"The rodeo announcer?"

"And the worst offender—you." Rachel pointed at Clint but snatched her hand back when the tip of her fingernail scraped his bare chest.

"You're talking nonsense."

Good Lord, she wished he'd step aside and give her breathing room. "There you go again, cutting me down. Whittling away at my self-confidence. Making fun of my—"

Giving no thought to the consequences, Clint leaned inside the truck and kissed Rachel. *Strawberry.* Her lip gloss tasted like fresh fruit—sweet and succulent. He'd only meant to silence her but the longer his mouth remained on hers the stronger the warm current that flowed from her lips to his. When Rachel didn't protest, Clint tilted his head and tried a different angle. Same result—more heat. The warmth spread through his gut, causing his jeans to become uncomfortably tight. Rachel sighed and set her hand against his chest, her nails biting into Clint's flesh. Startled, he snapped out of his reverie and staggered back. What the hell had gotten into him? He'd almost stuck his tongue into her mouth.

Pressing her fingertips to her swollen lips, she mumbled, "What did you do that for?"

"To stop your babbling."

"I was not babbling."

"Then cut to the chase and tell me what happened." Clint added another foot of space between them, hoping distance would help cool off his body.

Keeping her gaze averted, Rachel explained. "Lauren answered the phone today and let it slip that P.T. is in Phoenix undergoing cancer treatments."

Oh, boy. He'd told his daughter P.T.'s condition was a secret. Typical teen—in one ear and out the other.

"A few minutes ago Mayor McDonnell threatened to cancel the Canyon City Rodeo. Then the mayor of Boot Hill called and—"

"Why do they want to cancel?"

"They believe once word of P.T.'s condition spreads, the top competitors will withdraw and choose other rodeos to ride in, and attendance will drop, which means less revenue for the towns' businesses."

Shit. Clint kept his thoughts to himself, but agreed with the mayors. Cowboys competed in the rodeos where earnings were guaranteed. If the sponsors balked because P.T. wasn't running the show then the cowboys would become nervous and move on to surer money. If the top competitors scratched their rides, the stock contractors would pull out and the whole damn ball of wax would melt.

"What did the mayor of Piney Gorge have to say?" Clint asked, wishing Rachel would make eye contact.

"He feels the same. The mayors agreed to reconsider canceling the rodeos if I brainstorm an idea guaranteed to beat last year's ticket sales, which should prevent the popular cowboys from withdrawing."

"What happens if you fail?"

"Mayor McDonnell said he'd replace the rodeo with a carnival."

If P.T. had put Clint in charge this mutiny would never have occurred. "What's your plan?"

Her gaze clashed with his. "I don't have a plan. That's why I came out here in the sweltering sun…to ask *you* what we should do."

"We should talk to P.T. and see if he has any suggestions."

Rachel bolted from the truck then faced Clint, hands on her hips. "My father doesn't need to know about this."

"Why the hell not? It's his rodeo company."

"He has enough to worry about with his health. He doesn't need the added stress of wondering whether or not his rodeos will be canceled."

"You're in over your head, Rachel."

"This isn't my fault," she said. "Lauren's the one who—"

"You're a schoolteacher, not a—"

"Psychologist."

"Whatever. You don't know a damned thing about producing a rodeo."

"I realize that."

"You should have turned P.T. down when he asked for your help."

"My father, whom I haven't spoken with in over two years, calls me out of the blue with the news he has cancer and needs my help." She crossed her arms over her chest. "Would you have said no?"

Score a point for Rachel. Clint reined in his temper. "I don't get it. You've ignored P.T. most of your life and suddenly out of the goodness of your heart you want to help him?"

"Do you know why we've been estranged?" she asked.

No. "P.T. doesn't talk about you very often."

She sucked in a quiet breath. "Then you shouldn't judge me."

"You're right." Clint didn't know what it felt like to be alienated from a parent. He'd never met his birth mother or father, and he'd never experienced a meaningful connection with any of his foster parents. P.T. was the only adult Clint had formed a bond with. It was because of that bond that Clint resisted the urge to stand back and watch Rachel fail.

"I've busted my backside on this ranch for years, as well as helped P.T. with his rodeos." He paced alongside the truck. "I know the sponsors, the vendors and the cowboys—they trust me. No matter what scheme you invent to sell tickets, the mayors won't give you a chance because you're an outsider."

"So I'm destined to fail." Rachel's shoulders slumped.

"P.T.'s counting on me to help you succeed. If you don't, then I take the blame." Clint spread his arms wide. "Either way I'm screwed."

"You're worried about your own ass."

More than his ass was at stake. "At the end of the summer you'll pack your bags and return to your life on the East Coast—" he hoped "—while I remain here figuring out how to recoup the lost revenue."

"There might be a way to fix this," she said. "We tell the mayors that you're managing the rodeos."

Clint clenched his jaw until pain splintered through the bone.

"If the mayors believe you're the front man they'll stop panicking and I'll be able to concentrate on ticket sales."

"Fine. Tell them I'm in charge."

"Maybe you have a few ideas to increase attendance."

"I don't." He'd play his role in Rachel's little white lie with the mayors if only to appease P.T.'s request that he help his daughter. But Clint refused to throw her a life vest and devise a scheme to increase ticket sales. Rachel could sink or swim on her own.

"What should I say when people call and ask for you?"

"Tell them I'm busy and that you'll take a message and get back to them with my answer," Clint said.

"That won't fly unless you attend the meeting with the mayors on Monday and assure them you're making the decisions."

"Okay, I'll be there. Any other crisis I need to handle for you?"

"Nope. That's it for today." Chin high, Rachel got in her truck and shifted into Reverse, narrowly missing the bumper of Clint's vehicle.

Get a grip on yourself, man.

If Clint wasn't arguing with the woman, he was kissing her.

He doubted P.T. had that in mind when he'd assigned Clint the task of assisting his daughter.

RACHEL GLANCED IN THE rearview mirror and glared at Clint until the dust from the truck tires blocked him from view. The cowboy was an enigma. One minute he appeared willing to help, the next he avoided anything to do with promoting the rodeos. If she didn't know any better she'd believe Clint wanted her to fail, but why? She wasn't any threat to him. Besides, he had to realize that no good would come from canceling the rodeos—not if he intended to keep the sanctuary ranch in the black.

Maybe you're reading too much into the situation. Ever since her ex-fiancé's betrayal, Rachel had become overly suspicious of men's motives.

But boy, could Clint kiss.

She puckered her lips but the action did nothing to stop her mouth from tingling. If his kiss hadn't caught her by surprise she might have protested.

Yeah, right.

No sense pretending she hadn't fantasized about kissing Clint. Closing her eyes at bedtime and imagining him sweeping her into his arms and making love to her mouth had been the only thing that had saved her from a total nervous breakdown this week.

She'd been kissed by plenty of men. First-date kisses, which were always awkward. Second-date kisses weren't much better. And then there had been the welcome-neighbor kiss she'd received from the guy next door the day she'd moved into her condo. The teacher's-lounge kiss from the baseball coach who'd been in the middle of a divorce and had been feeling horny. And her former fiancé Mike's kisses, which had been pleasant, familiar—unlike Clint's kiss which had sizzled with heat.

Don't make a big deal out of the kiss. You enjoyed it because...because... Because it had been two years since Mike had met and fallen madly in love with a hotel maid while on a business trip to Japan and Rachel had yet to become involved with another man—not because she was stuck on Mike, but because she didn't trust her judgment when it came to men.

If Clint hadn't touched her cheek when he'd kissed her she wouldn't have been affected as deeply. But he had touched her, brushing the callused pad of his thumb against her skin. The tender caress had tugged at her heartstrings and a deep-seated need to be cherished.

The cowboy was hardly the kind of man to *cherish* a woman.

She'd never find out because Clint had kissed her to shut her up, not because he'd been unable to resist her allure. Shoving aside further thoughts about the cowboy, Rachel decided to brainstorm ideas for a rodeo PR campaign while she drove into town to grab a bite to eat. She made a pit stop at the house to grab her purse, then sped off. Once she reached town she picked the first bar that came into view— Gilly's Tap House.

Rachel entered the tavern, hovering in the

doorway until her eyes adjusted to the dim interior. The air conditioner mounted on the wall by the door blasted her face with cold air.

"If you're eating, menus are on the table," the barkeep called out.

Grabbing a laminated menu as she passed by a table, Rachel slid onto a bar stool near four women dressed in authentic cowgirl gear. She perused the menu. No salads.

"Decided yet?" The bald-headed barkeep stopped in front of her.

"I'll take an order of chicken fingers and fries, please."

"Care for a drink?"

"Ice water's good, thanks."

The bartender delivered her water then disappeared into the kitchen. While Rachel waited for her meal she studied the women at the bar. They looked average height but the leather chaps, big belt buckles and spurs made them appear larger than life.

Not wanting to get caught gaping, Rachel removed a pen and notebook from her purse. She refused to leave the bar until she thought of at least five ideas to promote the summer rodeos.

1. Place ad in newspapers within a hundred-mile radius of each town.

Not cheap, but not as expensive as canceling the rodeos.

2. Drawing for a new truck.

Who's going to donate a brand-new truck? Tomorrow she'd visit every dealership in Yuma and beg them to give away one of last year's models.

3. Offer a portion of the ticket sales to a charity.

What charity? These days there were so many causes it was difficult to find a charity a majority of people supported.

4. Bring in a halftime show.

How would she pay the performers? P.T. hadn't budgeted money for extras. Besides, thanks to Clint she was already overpaying the rodeo secretary.

5.

Rachel tapped the tip of the pen against the pad and stared into space. The door opened and another cowgirl walked into the bar, ordered a longneck and joined her friends. "We're out," the woman said.

Rachel eavesdropped.

"What do you mean, out?" one of the other cowgirls asked.

"They canceled our event."

The blond-haired cowgirl popped off her stool. "Why? We ride bulls as well as any cowboy on the circuit."

The women were bull riders?

"Same old excuse. Can't find enough of us to compete and we're a liability."

"That's stupid. Cowboys don't sue when they fall off a bull and get hurt."

As the women bantered, a fifth idea sparked in Rachel's mind. The barkeep set her chicken fingers and fries in front of her, then moved across the room and played a game of darts. Leaving her meal untouched, Rachel interrupted the women. "Excuse me, but I couldn't help overhearing you ladies ride bulls?"

Five heads bobbed up and down.

"You're all professional rodeo athletes?"

"Yes and no." The redhead spoke. "We have regular jobs but on weekends we rodeo. We took off today to practice for the Sierra Vista Rodeo this weekend, but Shannon said they canceled the women's rough-stock event."

"Riding bulls is a hobby, then?" Rachel asked.

"Not for me," the brunette said.

Rachel offered her hand. "I'm Rachel Lewis."

"Shannon Douglas." The cowgirl had beautiful green eyes. "I work as a ranch hand on a local spread but my main goal is to make a name for myself in women's bull riding."

"I had no idea women rode bulls." Rachel couldn't imagine any woman wanting to sit on the back of a raging bull.

"I'm Skylar Riggins," the blonde said, then pointed to the redhead. "Kim Beaderman..." The finger moved to the petite woman. "Wendy Chin." Next to where Wendy sat, "Julie Kenner."

"We're not as accomplished at the sport as Shannon is," Skylar said.

Rachel was fascinated. "Where do you work when you're not rodeoing?"

Skylar spoke first. "I'm a records transcriptionist for the medical center in Yuma."

"I process insurance claims," Wendy said.

"And I teach second grade at an elementary school in Yuma," Kim added.

Julie spoke next. "I'm a paralegal."

"I'm a school psychologist from Rhode Island," Rachel said. "Visiting my father for the summer. Would you mind if I ask a few more questions?"

"What do you want to know?" Shannon asked.

"How much money do women make at bull riding?"

"Not anywhere near as much as the men," Shannon said.

"We're not in it for the money." Skylar motioned to Shannon. "But Shannon's made some money riding."

"I ride bulls because I believe women can

do it as well as men if they're given a chance," Shannon said. Rachel sensed there was more to Shannon's reason than equal rights among cowboys and cowgirls.

"What do the cowboys think of you ladies competing against them?"

"We don't compete with the men, but there are few women who ride bulls, which makes it tough to find events to ride in."

The more information she gleaned from the women, the more excited Rachel became. "How many women do you have to have for an event?"

"At least six," Wendy chimed in.

"Would you be willing to compete in a rodeo if the payoff was small?" Rachel asked.

"I'd trade in my winnings any day for more publicity," Shannon said.

Rachel grinned. "Well, ladies, I'd like to make you an offer."

"What's that?" Skylar asked.

"How would you like to compete in the Canyon City Rodeo on Saturday, June twentieth?"

"Are you serious?" Shannon's eyes sparkled.

"Very serious. Five Star Rodeos is promoting the event, as well as two other rodeos—one in July and one in August." Rachel looked at Shannon. "Can you find another cowgirl to ride by next Saturday?"

"I guarantee it," Shannon said.

"And all of you will help spread the word about the event?" Rachel asked the other women.

Kim elbowed Skylar in the side. "We'll use our jobs to promote the event and our Facebook and Twitter accounts. Shannon has over fifty thousand Facebook friends and hordes of fans who follow her blog about rodeo."

"I'll check with the PTA moms at school to see if they can afford to sponsor an end-of-year field trip and take the kids to the rodeo," Kim said.

"Are you willing to be interviewed by the media?" Rachel asked.

"If you can get a newspaper reporter interested in me I'll talk their ear off and give a few colorful quotes," Shannon said.

Now all Rachel had to do was convince the mayor of Canyon City that a women's roughstock event would draw big crowds. Hopefully, if she succeeded in Canyon City, the mayors of Boot Hill and Piney Gorge would keep Five Star Rodeos on their calendar. Rachel flipped her notepad to a clean sheet of paper and passed it to Shannon. "Write down your names and cell numbers."

"You can have my firstborn if this works out," Shannon said.

"I'll be in touch, ladies." Eager to return to

the ranch and spill the beans to Clint, Rachel left the tavern but came to a screeching halt when she noticed Clint's daughter sitting behind a skanky-looking man on a Harley Davidson hog.

Chapter Six

Eyes on Clint's daughter, Rachel cut across the parking lot of Gilly's Tap House. "Lauren."

"Hey, Rachel."

Rachel studied the Harley thug. She guessed his age to be at least forty if not forty-five. His frizzy brown hair fell to the middle of his chest and tattoos covered his neck, arms and the backs of his hands. An array of metal rings pierced his eyebrows, nose and lip. Mirrored sunglasses concealed his eyes. He flashed a toothy grin, mocking her perusal.

"I don't believe I caught your name," Rachel said.

The brute removed his shades to reveal beady dark eyes. Rachel didn't flinch. She'd dealt with teenage gangsters before and learned never to show fear.

"Rocky," the man said.

"Rocky what?"

He chuckled. "Rocky Balboa."

Smart-ass. Clint should keep better tabs on his daughter. "Hop off the bike, Lauren."

"Rocky's taking me into Yuma to get a new tattoo."

"Did your father give you permission?"

"I'm eighteen. I don't need my dad's okay for anything. Besides—" Lauren inched her mini-skirt higher to reveal a picture of a butterfly on her hip "—I already have a tatt."

Okay, so Clint didn't care if his daughter had a tattoo. "Does your father know you left the ranch with Rocky?"

"Is this gonna take long?" Rocky groaned.

"Yes."

"No."

Rachel and Lauren spoke in unison. Rocky set the bike's kickstand and fiddled with the buttons on his leather vest, aligning the swastikas in the same direction.

"I was bored, so I walked to the road and hitched a ride into town." Lauren pointed across the lot. "I would have driven myself but you took the truck."

Typical teenager—blame everyone else for their bad decisions. "Mel said he's having trouble getting the paint color for the Prius." Why was Rachel defending herself? She had a right to drive her father's vehicle.

"Rocky'll bring me home before dark." Lauren nudged the man's meaty shoulder. "Right?"

Good guy or not, *Rocky* needed to find a friend his own age. Rachel removed the notepad from her purse and scribbled down the bike's license plate number. "You leave this parking lot with her and I'll file a missing persons report. You won't make it halfway to Yuma before the highway patrol arrests you for kidnapping."

"This bites." Lauren climbed off the bike. "You're not my legal guardian."

Rocky revved the Harley engine then tore out of the parking lot, spewing bits of gravel and dust into the air. "You're a very fortunate young lady, Lauren."

"Really? How's that?"

"Rocky was a bad seed and could have easily held you against your will and had his way with you or left you for dead in the desert."

"I thought you were cool because you liked my hair, but it was all an act, wasn't it?" Without giving Rachel a chance to reply, Lauren stuck her iPod earbuds in and headed for the truck.

Relieved she'd extricated Clint's daughter from the clutches of Satan's helper, Rachel drove back to the ranch. When she parked in front of the house her cell phone went off. "We'll discuss this later," Rachel said.

Lauren slammed the truck door and stormed off. "Hello?"

"Rachel?"

"Dad?" Surprised to hear her father's voice, she asked, "Is everything all right?"

"I'm fine. Thought I'd see if any problems cropped up with the Canyon City Rodeo."

Rachel's breath caught. Had Clint informed P.T. that news of his condition had leaked out and the mayors were threatening to pull the plug on their hometown rodeos? "Everything's going as planned." She crossed her fingers.

"Good to hear. Remember, if you run into a snag, Clint will help."

Her go-to man was fast becoming her run-away man.

"Clint's been a godsend to me through the years."

P.T.'s words triggered an ache in her chest. She doubted he realized when he bragged about Clint, he twisted the knife in her heart a little deeper.

"Rest assured things are running smoothly." *Change the subject.* "When do your radiation treatments begin?"

"Tomorrow." A forlorn sigh drifted into Rachel's ear.

Through the years P.T. had failed her on many levels, but he was still a human being and she worried about him. "I plan to visit you this Sunday."

"I don't want any visitors. You stay there and take care of business."

Darned if she'd beg.

"Rachel." P.T. cleared his throat.

"Yes?"

"I'm asking a lot—"

"Stop fretting about the rodeos, Dad. Take care of yourself and do what the doctors say."

"You sound like your mother when you scold me. Talk to you soon." P.T. disconnected the call. When Rachel stepped from the truck she came face-to-face with a scowling Clint.

"What did you do to upset Lauren?"

"She's mad that I wouldn't allow her to ride into Yuma with her new friend."

"I'm her father. You have no business telling Lauren what she can and cannot do."

"If you'd acted like her father instead of her best friend I wouldn't have had to intervene today."

"What are you talking about?"

"I ran into Lauren at Gilly's Bar."

"You drove the old truck and the Prius is still in the shop, so how did Lauren get into town?"

"She walked to the highway and hitched a ride with a creep on a Harley."

Clint's face turned ashen.

"Was she drinking at Gilly's?"

"No, but I stopped her from going with Rocky to get a new tattoo."

The nerve along Clint's jaw pulsed.

"What Lauren did was dangerous and immature. If you don't set boundaries with her she'll end up in a situation she can't handle and one you can't rescue her from."

"Don't tell me how to discipline my daughter. You don't know anything about our situation."

"I've seen your *situation* a hundred times over in my experience working with teenagers."

"Oh, yeah?"

"You feel guilty for not being there for Lauren most of her life, so instead of being a real father, you're trying to be her friend so she thinks you're cool."

"That's ridiculous."

"Okay, then, how will you handle Lauren's hitchhiking? What's her punishment?"

Clint whipped off his hat and shoved his fingers through his hair. "For God's sake, Rachel, the girl's bored out her mind. So she made a mistake. I'll talk to her about it and she won't do it again. End of story."

Rachel sympathized with the teen's predicament—stuck on a ranch for the summer without friends. "If she's bored, make her help with chores. Don't allow her to sit around all day complaining."

"She's a girl. That's what girls do—complain."

"You're making excuses for her because you don't want to play the heavy."

"This discussion is over." Clint took two steps before Rachel's voice stopped him.

"Don't you want to hear about my idea to increase ticket sales?"

She'd saved his daughter from making a grave mistake—the least he could do is let her bend his ear. "What idea?"

"Five Star Rodeos is going to promote a women's rough-stock event alongside the men's competition."

"What event?"

"Bull riding."

Rachel was nuts. Between controlling his daughter and supervising business activities, the noose around Clint's neck tightened a notch. "Do you have any idea what you're getting into?"

"How difficult can it be to add one more event to the schedule?"

He kicked a clump of dirt with the toe of his boot. "Where are you going to find enough women willing to ride bulls?"

"Five cowgirls signed on already and they promised to find one more before the rodeo."

"I assume you ran into these women at Gilly's?"

"Yep."

"Were they drunk?"

"No. They ride bulls for fun, but one is a serious contender. Shannon—"

"Douglas?"

Rachel nodded. "She's a ranch hand in the area."

Clint knew of Shannon Douglas. The young woman was making a name for herself in bull riding and never missed an opportunity to promote the sport. "Who are the other women?"

Rachel dug out her notebook from her purse. "Kim Beaderman. She teaches second grade in Yuma. Skylar Riggins is a medical transcriptionist. Wendy Chin works for an insurance company and Julie Kenner is a paralegal."

"What were they doing at a bar on a Friday afternoon?"

"They took the day off to practice for the rodeo in Sierra Vista but Shannon said the promoters canceled the women's bull-riding event at the last minute."

"And you offered to sponsor a competition for them."

"I'll phone the stock contractor tomorrow

and ask him to bring a few extra bulls for the women to ride," Rachel said.

"It doesn't work like that."

She crossed her arms over her chest and tapped her foot against the ground. "Then *you* tell me how it works."

"The bulls women ride aren't as tough and wild as the ones you see in the men's competition."

"I don't understand."

"The men ride twenty-two to twenty-three-point bulls. The animals are scored according to their meanness and killer instinct. In women's bull riding they use seventeen- to nineteen-point bulls. The bulls are screened carefully to make sure they won't turn on a fallen rider." The further he explained, the paler Rachel's face became. "Most stock contractors won't invest in raising bulls for women's events because there's no money in it."

"We don't need special bulls. Shannon said she's as good as any cowboy who—"

"I'm aware of the woman's talent, but she doesn't have the same level of experience as guys who've just graduated from high school."

"What do you mean?"

"After mutton bustin' competitions there's no organized women's rough-stock events in high school or college. When Shannon began competing she didn't have anywhere near the hours of practice on bulls as male competitors her age. And because few rodeos sponsor saddle-bronc or bull riding for women, it's tough for Shannon to gain the experience she needs to ride a twenty-three point bull."

"You're saying people wouldn't pay to watch women ride bulls?"

"I'm telling you that you'll have a problem getting P.T.'s stock contractor to agree to bring bulls for a women's event."

"I believe rodeo fans will travel a long way to watch a group of brave women ride bulls," Rachel said. "Once the mayors are on board with the plan, the stock contractor will be forced to cooperate."

P.T. put Rachel in charge. If she was dead set on adding women's bull riding to the schedule, so be it. Clint wasn't having any part of it. "You're in charge, so I'll leave you to your business."

"Clint, wait."

Now what?

"Remember, we're telling the mayors that you're running the rodeos, which means the women's bull-riding event has to be your idea."

Peeved that P.T. had put him in this position and doubly ticked that he couldn't control his daughter, Clint grasped at straws. "I'll get the mayors to sign on to the idea in exchange for a favor." Why the heck was he having trouble keeping his gaze off Rachel's mouth?

His stare must have unnerved her because she licked her lips. "What do I have to do?"

"Let Lauren help with the rodeos."

"She won't want to do menial office work."

"She will when she learns she has a choice of working for you or going without her iPod, movies and magazines."

"That's how you discipline—shove your child off on someone else?"

"You want my help or not?" Clint asked.

"I suppose she could file papers and take phone messages."

"Then it's settled." What the hell had he done to deserve all this female aggravation? Clint screwed his hat on tight and headed for the cabin and his next showdown—Lauren.

"LAUREN!" CLINT BELLOWED as soon as he opened the cabin door. He skidded to a halt when he noticed his daughter seated at the kitchen table, listening to her iPod.

She shut off the gadget, removed her earbuds and glowered. "What?"

"We need to talk."

Lauren rolled her eyes in that aggravating

teenage way that made Clint want to grind his teeth.

"You left the ranch without telling me."

"I shouldn't have agreed to stay here this summer."

Clint let her believe she'd had a say in the decision.

Lauren bolted from the chair. "I'm tired of listening to music. Tired of watching DVDs. Tired of reading. Tired of sleeping. Tired of staring at the walls." She shook her fist. "Tired of this stupid, hot desert!"

Keeping his frustration in check, Clint said, "That's no excuse for making bad choices."

"I wouldn't have hitched a ride with Rocky if I'd believed he was going to rape me."

An image of his daughter lying in the desert beaten and left for dead flashed before Clint's eyes. Where the heck was Lauren's common sense? Good thing he hadn't allowed her to remain in Los Angeles this summer. God only knows what she would have tried to get away with.

"Rocky was harmless, Dad."

"Maybe he was. But what about the next guy you sneak off with? He might be a serial killer."

"You act like I hitch rides every day!"

"You're my daughter. I care about what happens to you." He raised a hand when she opened her mouth to protest. "I also realize you're an adult and you'll make decisions I don't agree with."

His comment took the steam out of Lauren's mad and she sank onto the chair seat. He joined her at the table. "I'm sorry you got stuck here this summer. I know it isn't very exciting and you miss your friends."

Tears welled in Lauren's eyes, making Clint feel even worse. "But that being said, bad decisions have consequences."

She studied him warily. "What kind of consequences?"

"You pick your punishment. Help Rachel with the rodeos or lose your TV, iPod and magazines for the summer."

"You're kidding, right?"

"I'm dead serious. I paid for your iPod. I pay the TV bill and I paid for your fashion-magazine subscription."

"You want me to be miserable."

"I want you to learn to make reasonable, safe, mature decisions and not jump on the back of a Harley with a stranger."

"What do I have to do for Rachel?"

"She didn't say. You'll have to work out the details with her." Silence filled the kitchen. "What's it going to be? Grounded for the rest of the summer or help with the rodeos?"

"Like that's even a choice?" She snorted. "I guess I'm helping Rachel." Lauren flashed a smug smile. "Maybe I'll meet some cute cowboys at the rodeos."

Great. Now Clint had to worry about his daughter sneaking off to the horse barn with a wet-behind-the-ears bronc rider. He narrowed his eyes. "Don't push me."

"Whatever. Are we through discussing this?"

He let her off the hook. "Have you heard from your mom lately?" he asked.

"She emailed last night and said she's having fun."

Clint was sure his daughter had written back that she hated being at the ranch.

"Anything else?" Lauren snapped.

"Nope. I think we've covered everything."

As soon as Lauren left the kitchen Clint breathed a sigh of relief. Their talk had gone better than expected. Deciding to vent his frustration on the hay bales that needed moving in the loft, Clint left the cabin. Halfway to the barn, Rachel's voice stopped him. She sat on the bench beneath the piñon tree, murmuring to P.T.'s cat.

"I see you made friends with Felix," he said.

"He misses P.T." Rachel stroked the cat's head.

Clint edged closer and leaned a shoulder

against the tree trunk. "Felix wandered onto the ranch years ago. P.T. figured he'd been dumped by the road."

"People can be so cruel to animals." She scooted over and patted the empty space beside her. "Have a seat."

The seat was barely big enough for one, but his boots had a mind of their own and he joined her on the bench. Rachel's scent floated on the breeze—faded perfume, sunscreen and her own unique essence. He wiggled, attempting to put a few extra inches of space between them, but failed.

Ignoring the warm contact where their thighs rubbed, he said, "I spoke with Lauren. She's reporting for duty tomorrow morning."

"Bet she was thrilled."

Clint let her comment slide and listened to a coyote's cry echoing through the night.

"May I ask you a question?"

"Sure."

"You said my father rarely spoke of me."

"You came up in conversation a few times through the years."

"What did he say?"

"P.T. mentioned that you'd broken your wrist."

Rachel had fallen off her bike at a friend's house in seventh grade. "What else?"

"He was excited when you graduated in the top three percent of your high-school class."

P.T. had never told her he was proud of her academic achievements. He'd signed her graduation card *Regards, Your Father.*

"Did P.T. attend your high-school graduation?"

"Yes." He heard her draw a sharp breath but she dropped the subject.

"Lauren said you were in foster care."

"My daughter talks too much."

"I'd like to hear about your experience…if you're willing to share."

"I ran away from my foster home at sixteen. Mr. and Mrs. Kipling were a weird couple."

"How so?"

"They didn't have any children of their own and were members of the Church of All Worlds, which was more cult than religion."

"Did they mistreat you?"

"No. But one day I walked in the door after school to a houseful of naked people worshipping faerie statues and twirling magic wands." He'd decided he'd had enough of the Kiplings' craziness and had packed his meager belongings and hit the road.

"Why didn't you report the foster parents to your caseworker?"

"I did but my complaints were ignored. Too

many kids and not enough homes to place them in. I was told to stop complaining and be happy I had a roof over my head."

"How did you make it this far west?"

"Hitched rides with truckers." Fearful of drawing suspicion and being turned over to authorities, Clint had hiked through the desert, hoping to cross undetected into Mexico.

"I cut through P.T.'s property and took shelter in the barn." The hot desert had exhausted him. "P.T. found me the next morning asleep in a horse stall."

"My father didn't call the sheriff?"

"I begged him not to." Clint had refused to reveal his name, age or where he'd lived for fear of being returned to Phoenix. "I offered to work for room and board but after a week I broke down and told P.T. I'd run from my foster home."

"Then he phoned the sheriff."

"No, he contacted social services and asked what he had to do to become a foster parent." P.T. had spent hours completing paperwork, being interviewed and attending special classes. Once he'd been approved he became Clint's official foster parent and the rest was history.

"Things worked out better than you'd hoped for, I guess."

"If I'd been sent back to Phoenix I'd have

ended up in a juvenile detention center for run-away delinquents." Thinking about that year in his life, he figured if P.T. hadn't agreed to raise him, Clint would have run again, only this time he would have made it across the border and who knows what fate had awaited him in Mexico.

"Why didn't you attend college?"

"I enjoyed helping P.T. with the rodeos so I joined the circuit after high school."

"You were a rodeo cowboy?"

"Bull rider."

"I guess you do know a little bit about bull riding. So you returned to Five Star Ranch after you quit rodeoing."

"I never really left. I helped P.T. with chores during the week and competed in events on weekends. Nothing changed when I retired from the circuit and became a bullfighter."

"You mean a rodeo clown?"

"The politically correct term is bullfighter. These days bullfighters wear bright, loose-fitting athletic shorts and T-shirts designed to tear away if the bull's horn snags the material."

"Did you use clown makeup?" She smiled, trying to picture this macho man with white powder covering his face, a big red dot on each cheek.

"Yep."

"I don't know who's crazier, a cowboy who rides a bull or one who toys with a bull."

"Unlike a bull rider, the bullfighter always collects a paycheck at the end of the night."

"Do you still bullfight?" she asked.

"On occasion. Back when the economy hit a rough patch, P.T. was worried about paying for your grad school." He shrugged. "I worked the rodeo circuit that year and brought in extra income to keep the feed bins full."

Rachel wasn't sure how she felt about Clint's confession. She didn't like the idea that he'd returned to a dangerous job in a roundabout way because of her. "P.T. never defaulted on my loans."

"He took out a second mortgage on the ranch to pay off your college bills."

If her father cared enough about her to mortgage his ranch, then why on earth hadn't he made an effort to establish a relationship with her?

Clint fidgeted, acting as if he wanted to leave. Rachel wanted him to stay. "How often do you see Lauren?" She felt guilty for attacking Clint's parenting skills earlier. After learning he'd been raised in foster care then taken in by P.T., who had pretty much ignored his own daughter through the years, was it any wonder Clint struggled with parenting?

"Lauren and I talk on the phone twice a month but we haven't seen a lot of each other through the years. P.T. pushed me to visit Lauren more often, but she always made plans with her friends and Lauren's mother didn't force her to spend time with me."

Rachel found it ironic that P.T. had been concerned about what kind of father Clint was but hadn't held himself up to the same high standard. Interesting that she'd returned to Arizona seeking information about her and P.T.'s estranged relationship only to have more questions than answers.

Rachel gathered her courage to ask one final question. "Did P.T. ever say why he insisted I live with my aunt after my mother died?"

"P.T. sent you away? I thought you'd chosen to live with your aunt."

"Hardly."

"Is that why you agreed to help P.T. this summer—so you two could mend your fences?"

"Yes." Rachel slid off the bench and moved into the shadows. Clint might not be P.T.'s son by birth, but it was obvious her father cared more about his ranch foreman than his own daughter.

The truth was painful. On one hand Rachel wanted to hate Clint for stealing her father's attention through the years. On the other hand she sympathized with Clint's tumultuous childhood and was relieved he'd found someone who'd cared about him.

"I'd always pictured my father a lonely old man. I'm relieved he had you, Clint." The knowledge freed Rachel to let go of the guilt she'd carried as an adult because she hadn't remained in contact with her father.

Feeling raw and needy she said, "I'd better go inside." She stepped past Clint, but he grasped her hand. His warm callused fingers entwined with hers, sending shivers racing up her arm.

"I'm sorry P.T. didn't—"

"It's in the past. All that matters now is that P.T. recovers his health."

Clint squeezed her fingers, drawing Rachel's gaze to his face. The darkness concealed his eyes but his breathing grew ragged as short, hot puffs of air hit her face. If she turned her head just a tad, her mouth would graze his. Heart pounding, she yearned for his kiss, but common sense intervened at the last second and she broke contact.

"See you tomorrow." She scurried up the path and into the house, sliding the bolt across the door, wondering if she hoped to lock herself in or Clint out.

Chapter Seven

"My dad said I had to help you or he'd ground me." Lauren stood in the office doorway, a defiant glare on her face.

"I could use help making phone calls."

"You don't have to act like you want me here." Lauren plopped into the leather chair. "I know my dad's forcing me on you."

Rachel had to tread water carefully or the teen would throw a hissy fit and bolt. If she expected Clint's help with the mayors Monday afternoon, then she needed Lauren's cooperation.

"This rodeo stuff is so lame."

"I thought so, too, until I came up with an idea to increase attendance."

"What idea?"

"We're going to sponsor a women's rough-stock event."

"What's a rough-stock event?"

"Bull riding for women."

Lauren sat up straight. "Women ride bulls?"

"Who would've thought females were that crazy, huh?"

"Who are the girls?"

Relieved Lauren appeared excited about something, Rachel passed her notepad to Lauren. "I want you to call each of the women who've agreed to ride in the Canyon City Rodeo and ask them when they're available to do newspaper and radio interviews."

"Then what?"

"Then you phone the newspapers and radio stations in the area and set up interviews with the reporters."

"Cool."

"Before you contact the media outlets, find out all you can about the lady bull riders. Any tidbit of information that will entice a reporter to want to talk to them."

"You mean I'm sort of interviewing the women first?"

"Exactly."

"What kind of questions should I ask?"

"That's up to you. Whatever you think the reporters might find interesting."

"Um…maybe how many boyfriends they've had?"

Rachel stared.

"You know, 'cause some guys might be afraid

to date a girl who rides bulls. They could worry that she's tougher than they are."

Keeping a straight face, Rachel said, "Okay, go ahead and ask about their boyfriends."

"Do you have an extra notebook I can use to brainstorm questions?"

Rachel held out the brand-new leather-bound journal she'd found in her father's drawer.

"This looks expensive."

"You'll need to write down your contacts—reporters' names and cell numbers. Information about each bull rider. And you'll have to keep track of interview dates and times. Make reminder calls so the women don't forget to show up at the stations."

"Should I show you the questions I come up with before I ask the women?" Lauren paced in front of the desk, her eyes bright with excitement.

"Nope. I trust you."

"If it's okay, I'm going to go back to my room in the cabin and write stuff down."

"Lauren." Rachel spoke before the teen left the office. "I want the women to attend the meeting Monday afternoon with the mayors. Fran's Waffle House right off the interstate. Three o'clock. Maybe you can come up with a way for them to make a big splash with the townspeople."

"Why do they have to impress anyone?"

"Because most folks don't believe women should ride bulls."

"Why not?"

"They consider bull riding a man's sport."

"Are these women big and ugly?"

"No. As a matter of fact they're all attractive."

"I've got an idea, but it's a surprise." The teen fled the office.

Rachel relaxed after the front door shut. Things had gone better than she'd hoped with Lauren. Now all Clint had to do was live up to his end of the bargain and convince the mayors not to cancel their rodeos.

HEARTY BACKSLAPS AND zealous handshakes greeted Clint Monday afternoon when he stepped inside Fran's Waffle House on the outskirts of Canyon City. The restaurant was packed to the gills with citizens from the three towns Five Star Rodeos had contracted with.

The restless crowd urged Clint toward the back of the room where tables had been pushed together and behind which sat the mayors of Canyon City, Boot Hill and Piney Gorge. If Clint didn't know better he'd believe he was the guest of a celebrity roast. Too bad the only thing being toasted today was his arse.

"Good to see you, Clint." Mitch McDonnell motioned to the chairs on his right. "You know John Larsen and Jack Ross."

Clint gestured to the mayors, but his eyes remained riveted on the restaurant door. Rachel and Lauren were nowhere in sight. Evidently it was up to him alone to convince the townspeople to trust Five Star Rodeos.

Mayor McDonnell banged a gavel against the table and the crowd settled down. "Each of our towns has a stake in the success of their summer rodeo, so let's get down to business." Rumbles of agreement echoed through the room.

"The annual Canyon City Rodeo is scheduled to kick off this Friday. Last week I learned the sad news that P. T. Lewis, the owner of Five Star Rodeos, is battling cancer at one of those fancy hospice hospitals in Phoenix."

Murmurs of sympathy followed the mayor's statement.

Shoving his chair back, Clint stood. "Pardon the interruption, Mayor." McDonnell motioned Clint to continue. "For those of you who don't know me, I'm Clint McGraw—foreman of Five Star Ranch. I'd like to settle any misconceptions about P.T.'s health. He's not in a hospice facility and his prognosis is excellent."

Clint made eye contact with several people before continuing. "I understand the mayors are concerned news of P.T.'s health might adversely affect rodeo attendance numbers." He paused until the whispering stopped. "I've helped P. T. Lewis produce his rodeos for years, and this summer I'm in charge. I guarantee Five Star will put on a top-notch event for your town."

"I make most of my income for the year selling funnel cakes at the rodeo!" a woman shouted.

"I carve napkin rings for the craft show exhibit. I gotta sell enough rings to pay off my credit card!" another man added.

"I run the Sleep Tight Motel outside Piney Gorge. If I can't count on cowboys filling my rooms one weekend a summer I might as well burn the place down and collect the insurance money."

"You can't set your businesses on fire!" A short man with a big belly stood on a chair and shook his fist. "You'll put my insurance company out of business and I'll be forced to file for bankruptcy."

Mayor McDonnell smacked the gavel against the table, silencing the group. "There will be no talk of arson." The mayor removed a handkerchief from his trouser pocket and wiped his perspiring brow.

"I'm aware of the impact the rodeos have on your businesses and bottom line," Clint said.

"Nothing's going to change in the way we produce and promote the rodeos."

"If I might interject." The mayor of Boot Hill stood. "Last night I received a call from C. J. Rodriguez."

Rodriguez was a local rodeo legend who enjoyed convincing others that the world revolved around him. He'd made it to the National Finals Rodeo twice but had yet to win the buckle. Most riders of his caliber passed over small-town rodeos, but C.J. loved being the center of attention and the mayors made a big deal out of his presence—last year Piney Gorge presented Rodriguez a key to their town.

"C.J. heard about P.T.'s health problems," Mayor Ross continued, "and threatened to withdraw from the bronc-bustin' competition if we can't guarantee a decent-size purse and crowd."

Greedy bastard. If C.J. snubbed the rodeos then other top contenders would follow his lead.

"We gotta draw big crowds so C.J.'ll ride." The shout came from the rear of the room. "Folks don't wanna watch a *nobody* ride."

Intent on putting fears to rest, Clint said, "I'll contact C.J. and assure him that there will be a hefty-size purse and plenty of fans to cheer him on."

"Won't be the same without P.T. sitting in the

VIP section." Bob Casey, owner of the Watershed Bar in Piney Gorge, stood. "If it wasn't for P.T. bragging about my margaritas, folks wouldn't go out of their way to stop at my place after the rodeo."

McDonnell motioned for silence. "I've spoken with P.T.'s daughter and she'll be here any minute to present a plan to increase attendance and downplay the fact that P.T. won't be present at the rodeos."

"P.T. has a daughter?" A woman several feet away asked.

"Rachel Lewis came all the way from Rhode Island to spend the summer at P.T.'s ranch," Clint said.

"Rhode Island?" A man guffawed. "What does an easterner know about promoting rodeos?"

Not much. "Rachel's not promoting the events," Clint lied. "She's answering the phones and contacting people for me."

"She's your secretary?" Mayor Larsen asked.

"Something like that," Clint mumbled.

"Is she here?" McDonnell glanced around.

Dang it, Rachel. Where are you? Before Clint blurted an excuse for her absence, the waffle house door opened and in strolled Rachel, Lauren and six cowgirls dressed for a Hollywood movie audition. The lady bull riders sported tight jeans, sequined shirts, sparkly belt buckles, big hair and glittery makeup. Lauren remained by the door as Rachel led her entourage through the crowd—the mouths of men dropping open as the cowgirls passed by.

"I thought you were going to be a no-show," Clint whispered when Rachel stopped in front of the table. The scent of her perfume sent his thoughts careening back to the kiss they'd shared in the front seat of his truck. "Folks, allow me to introduce P.T.'s daughter, Rachel Lewis."

Several *Howdys* echoed through the crowd.

Clint motioned to the mayors. "This is John Larsen, mayor of Piney Gorge. Jack Ross, mayor of Boot Hill, and Mitch McDonnell, mayor of Canyon City."

Rachel shook hands with the men.

"Folks," Clint spoke to the group, "I've decided to add a new event this year to the rodeos because I believe it will increase attendance and stir up excitement in the community. Rachel will tell you all about it."

Rachel took center stage, looking downright Western in a pair of brand-new jeans, a flower-print cotton blouse and a flashy silver belt that accentuated her trim waist. Her small frame reminded Clint that a man would have to be careful making love to her—not that he had any intention of being that man. He shoved his lusty thoughts aside and listened to Rachel speak.

"Ladies and gentlemen, standing before you are six courageous and talented women," she said.

One of the men stuck his fingers in his mouth and whistled. The cowgirls preened. "You might ask yourself what these women have to do with promoting your rodeos—"

"Far as I'm concerned—" a geezer with a stringy beard spoke "—they got my permission to promote anything they want!" Hoots and hollers followed.

Clint removed the gavel from Mayor McDonnell's hand and banged the table.

"Everyone knows that rodeo is a dangerous sport where rough and tough men tame wild bulls and stubborn broncs." Heads in the crowd bobbed. "How many of you would pay to watch a woman ride a bull?"

No one raised their hand.

Rachel motioned to the cowgirls standing with her. "How many of you would pay to watch one of these ladies ride a bull?"

Every hand in the restaurant shot up in the air.

"Let me introduce you to the women who will be competing in their own bull-riding event at each of your rodeos." Rachel called off the women's names then opened the floor to questions. The men remained dumbstruck but not the women.

"Who made your fancy costumes?" a lady asked.

The petite blonde named Skylar Riggins stepped forward. "I did, ma'am."

"They're gorgeous. I sell hats and cowboy gear at the rodeos. Would you be interested in giving me a few of those shirts on consignment?"

"Yes, ma'am, I would."

"They've got my vote," the woman said.

"Before we get carried away," Mayor McDonnell said, "let's hear how Clint intends to promote the lady bull riders and why he believes their presence at the rodeo will increase ticket sales."

"Mitch, if you gotta be told why them gals will bring in more money, then your libido is malfunctioning and you ought to be takin' them tiny blue pills they advertise on TV." The men in the room chuckled.

Clint opened his mouth to speak but Rachel winked and cut him off. "Clint has secured a promise from these ladies to help advertise the event," Rachel said.

"Promote how?" someone asked.

"These talented women have successful careers outside of rodeo and will be using their places of employment to advertise the rodeos. Clint is working on securing TV and radio interviews as well as the possibility of offering free bull-riding lessons to females if they purchase a rodeo ticket."

"Great idea, Clint." A man in the back stepped forward. "I got a niece who'd be interested in them free lessons."

Amazed by the crowd's easy acceptance of a women's rough-stock event, Clint couldn't help but admire Rachel for her gutsy idea.

"For those of you who have computers, check out Shannon Douglas's blog 'Bull Ridin' ain't just for Boys,'" Rachel continued. "Shannon has thousands of followers and keeps her fans informed on where she's competing.

"This is Lauren McGraw, Clint's daughter." Rachel waved Clint's daughter to the front of the room. "Since Clint will be busy making sure the sponsors are following through on their pledges and working with the stock contractors to bring in the best rough stock for the events, Lauren and I will be helping out in the office. If you're interested in having any of these ladies promote your business, call the office and Lauren will relay your request to Clint. If he approves, Lauren will schedule a meeting to discuss the particulars."

"Missy." A woman pointed at Lauren's pink hair. "Is that a wig you're wearing?"

Clint winced, praying his daughter wouldn't overreact and shout a cuss word.

"This is my real hair." Lauren tugged a lock of pink hair.

The woman who'd voiced the question glanced at Clint. "Can I use her to promote my hair salon? I'll have a booth at the fairgrounds, advertising five-dollar haircuts, but I'd make more money coloring teenagers' hair."

"I'll wear a T-shirt at the rodeo advertising your salon." Lauren glanced at Clint. "If my dad says it's okay." What happened to the disgruntled teenager who wanted nothing to do with rodeo or the ranch?

With a curt nod Clint gave his permission and the hairstylist whooped.

"Hey, Clint. Do we gotta pay them gals extra if they promote our businesses?" a man called out.

"Sir." Shannon stepped forward. "If we can work your request into our schedules we'll endorse your business for free."

Heads in the audience bowed together as business owners brainstormed ideas on how to use the cowgirls to their advantage.

Mitch McDonnell banged the gavel on the

table. "All in favor of keeping Five Star Rodeos on their town's calendar..."

A chorus of *ayes* reverberated through the room.

Extricating himself from the crowd, Clint made a beeline for the exit. He needed a few minutes alone to come to grips with what had transpired—he'd arrived at the restaurant believing he hadn't had a chance in hell of convincing the mayors to buy into the idea of hosting a women's rough-stock event.

You were hoping, anyway.

Clint cursed the voice in his head. He admitted there had been a part of him that had wanted Rachel to fail if only to prove to P.T. he'd made a mistake putting his daughter in charge. Instead, the city girl had come through with flying colors. Damned if he didn't admire her for pulling off a miracle.

"Hey, Dad. There you are." Lauren joined his side. "Rachel put me in charge of handling the girls' social calendars. How cool is that?"

"Was that your idea in there?"

"What?"

"Having the women wear sexy clothes, big hair and glittery makeup?"

"Yeah. Pretty cool, huh?"

Whatever magic spell Rachel had cast over Lauren, he hoped it would last the summer.

Clint hadn't seen his daughter this animated in a long while.

"I've got Shannon scheduled for a radio interview next week." Lauren lowered her voice. "I told them I'd check with you first." She flipped open a notebook and showed Clint her chicken scratch. "Oh, and Rachel wanted me to ask if the women can ride bulls at the ranch."

"What?"

"Rachel said the bulls on the ranch are retired from rodeo."

Damn Rachel and her bright ideas.

"The girls are taking the day off from their jobs this Thursday to practice. Shannon said they can be there as early as seven in the morning."

"I don't know, Lauren. I've got a lot on my plate—"

"I'll help."

"Help how?"

"I'll muck the stalls in the barn." She tugged on his shirtsleeve. "C'mon, Dad. I've never seen a girl ride a bull."

"I don't have time to mess around with this kind of stuff."

"Forget it. Rachel and I will figure something out." Lauren stomped inside, leaving Clint to chew on his anger.

If P.T. wanted his estranged daughter in

charge of Five Star Rodeos, then Rachel could darn well start tackling her own problems. The more Clint helped her out the more she'd rely on him. He'd spent his entire adult life earning P.T.'s respect and admiration. He and P.T. had become family and damned if he'd allow Rachel to shove him aside and take his place without a fight.

"SHANNON'S AWESOME." Lauren stood with Clint outside the practice pen Thursday morning, watching the lady bull riders.

So much for holding his ground.

"Shannon has great balance." Clint watched the female athlete dust herself off.

For the past two days he'd ignored his daughter's nagging and Rachel's dark looks, but late last night he'd overheard Lauren telling her mother on the phone that she didn't want to be around her father anymore because he was a chauvinist pig. As much as Clint wanted Rachel to fail he didn't want to give his daughter another reason to avoid spending time with him. At 10:00 p.m. he'd turned on the outside lights and had constructed a holding pen for the bulls and a makeshift chute. Three hours later when he'd gone to bed, he'd found a note on his pillow. *Thanks, Dad. I knew you wouldn't let me and Rachel down.*

The message had triggered a session of painful self-examination. He'd lived in several foster homes where he'd been one of six or seven kids and had done whatever it took to rise above the fray to gain attention. Needing to be number one was normal for a kid, but he was thirty-seven years old. Would he ever let go of the little boy inside him who desperately wanted all the attention?

"Torpedo is one stubborn bull, Mr. McGraw," Shannon said.

"Only twelve cowboys ever made it to eight on Torpedo."

"Have you ever been hurt by a bull, Shannon?" Lauren asked.

"Heck, yes. I've broken my wrist twice, my ankle once and my fingers lots of times."

"Why do you keep riding?"

Clint knew why.

Shannon's attention remained on the chute where one of her friends prepared to ride Big Ben. "Ask any cowboy or cowgirl and they'll say they like the adrenaline rush they get from trying to tame two thousand pounds of—"

The chute door opened and Big Ben burst into the corral. The young woman stayed on for three seconds before flying off. She hit the ground and rolled to her feet with ease.

"—pure rage," Shannon continued. "But

not me. I'm riding bulls because they said I couldn't."

"Who said you couldn't?" Lauren asked.

"Men." Shannon glanced at Clint.

He grinned.

"I rode bulls with my brothers when I was young but every time I tried to sign in for a rodeo event they turned me away because I was a girl," Shannon said.

"That stinks," Lauren said.

"Thanks to your father—" Shannon smiled at Clint "—we have a chance to show rodeo fans that women bull riders deserve to be taken seriously." Shannon walked back to the chute.

"Dad?"

"What?"

"Would you let me ride bulls?"

"No." He held his breath waiting for an explosion.

Lauren's eyes rounded. "You're prejudiced against women."

"No, I believe women can do what a man does equally well, except ride bulls."

"No wonder Mom didn't want to marry you."

Ouch. "I'm not saying women aren't—"

"Forget it, Dad."

What happened to the grateful teen who left a nice note on his pillow?

Lauren stared over his shoulder and he turned

to see what had caught her attention. *Rachel.* For the first time since she'd arrived at the ranch she wore her blond hair loose, the thick strands falling a few inches past her shoulders. She looked fresh from the shower in her short denim skirt and sleeveless white blouse. Pink painted toenails peeked out of the strappy sandals covering her feet.

Where was she headed all gussied up?

"My dad thinks women shouldn't ride bulls," Lauren said when Rachel stopped at the pen.

"Why not?" Rachel stared at Clint.

"Because bulls are tough, mean, brutal beasts," he said.

"And…?" Rachel's smile zapped Clint in the chest.

"And women are soft—" his eyes zeroed in on the patch of creamy skin visible between the lapels of Rachel's shirt "—and delicate." He noticed a tiny freckle on her nose—the first of many he suspected would dot her porcelain complexion by the end of the summer. "And…" His gaze shifted to the fragile curve of her ear. He swallowed the word *sexy* and substituted "too smart to ride bulls."

Rachel snorted.

"Teach me how to ride bulls so I can tell all my friends back home that I competed in a rodeo."

"Not a chance, Lauren." Liz would have Clint's head if he allowed their daughter anywhere near a bull. "If you want to know what it feels like, try a bucking machine."

"Where am I going to find one of those?" Lauren asked.

"In the barn," Clint said. "I told Shannon she and her friends could use it whenever they wanted."

"Fine." Lauren jutted her chin. "I'll ask Shannon if she'll show me how to work the mechanical bull." Lauren walked off, leaving Clint alone with Rachel.

"You heading into town?" he asked.

"I'm paying my father a visit."

"Is everything all right with P.T.?" Clint had spoken with his boss last night, but P.T. hadn't mentioned any problems.

"As far as I know, he's fine, but he hasn't returned my calls."

Guilt flooded Clint. Rachel had asked him to notify her when P.T. phoned him and he'd forgotten. She'd be ticked if she knew her father had been in contact with him every day. Damned if he could figure out why P.T. had trouble reaching out to his daughter.

"P.T. doesn't want visitors," Clint said.

"I'm checking in on him anyway."

Obviously Rachel cared in some capacity for her father if she was taking the time to drive to Phoenix to see him. "Do me a favor?"

"Sure."

"Don't tell P.T. we've added a women's rough-stock event to the rodeos."

"Why not? The mayors are thrilled with my idea."

So it was *her* idea when they were alone and *his* when they were in public. He didn't care whose idea it was, he didn't want to risk looking bad in his mentor's eyes. "P.T.'s old-fashioned about some things and he isn't a big fan of women riding broncs or bulls."

"And you didn't see a need to mention this to me earlier?"

"Guess I forgot." P.T. would blame Clint for not putting a stop to Rachel's idea when he'd known his boss would disapprove. Right now the mayors were excited about the women's event but there were no guarantees the added attraction would be as successful as Rachel boasted.

"I'll be back late tonight," she said.

Clint reached into the front pocket of his jeans and removed his keys. "Use my truck." Damn Mel. The mechanic was taking forever to fix Rachel's Prius.

"The ranch truck is fine."

"I've got a GPS in mine. The Phoenix medical center is listed in My Favorites."

"I printed off directions from the internet."

Clint swore the woman was part mule.

"The tires on the ranch truck are old. I'd hate to see you stranded on the side of the road in hundred-degree heat." Every cowboy who passed by and caught a glimpse of her blond hair and short skirt would volunteer to change her flat and a whole lot more.

"Are you sure?"

"Positive."

"I'll reimburse you for gas."

Ignoring her offer, he said, "Tell P.T. that Lauren and I are thinking about him."

"I will."

Clint hung out at the corral, waiting for Rachel to leave. She made two trips into the house—one for a tote bag and another for a small cooler. A few minutes later she honked as she drove away. He decided she looked darn good sitting behind the wheel of his truck. Maybe there was a bit of cowgirl hidden inside the career woman.

Shannon shouted for help. Curly refused to enter the chute—damned stubborn bull. Like Clint, the bull was tired of bossy females.

THE MEDICAL CLINIC where P.T. received care was a modern facility with lots of windows. Rachel checked in at the front desk and received her father's room number. When she stepped off the elevator, the floor nurse informed her that P.T. was undergoing radiation treatment. Rachel was encouraged to make herself comfortable while she waited.

P.T. had a private room with a window overlooking a courtyard three floors below. The room was spacious enough to fit a hospital bed, a writing desk and a recliner. The walls were painted taupe—not the stark-white color or pale yellow common in many hospitals.

Nervous about her father's reaction to her visit, Rachel sat in the recliner. As she wiggled into a comfortable position an object poked her hip. She stuffed her hand beneath the cushion and pulled out P.T.'s eReader. Curious, she turned it on and discovered P.T. was reading *Planet Destiny*.

P.T. cared enough about Lauren to keep his promise and read the teen's science-fiction love story. She closed her eyes and imagined herself as a teenager. If she'd lived with P.T. back then, would he have shared her interest in the TV sitcom *Friends?* Would they have watched episodes together? Discussed the characters and laughed over the jokes?

A noise in the hallway caught her attention and she popped up from the chair. Her father entered the room, his face pale and drawn. Dressed in Western jeans and a long-sleeved shirt, he wore athletic shoes instead of cowboy boots.

His eyes widened when he noticed Rachel. "What are you doing here?"

Not the greeting she'd hope for. "Dad." The word sounded strangled and she cleared her throat. "Thought you might like company this afternoon."

"How long have you been waiting?" He sat on the side of the bed.

"Not long. How did your radiation treatment go?"

"I'd rather have gone to a rodeo."

"Are you hungry? Thirsty?"

"Stop fussing, daughter."

Rachel pulled out the desk chair and sat while P.T. reclined on the bed. "Everything set for the rodeo this Saturday?"

"There was one hiccup that had to be ironed out," she said.

P.T. frowned. "What happened?"

Clint advised her not to speak about the women's event. She assumed everything else was fair game. "Your rodeo secretary retired."

"Barb?"

"Her daughter had a baby and needed her help."

He motioned to the desk drawer. "Hand me my cell phone."

"No need. Nancy Smith agreed to work all three rodeos for Barb."

"Any other problems?"

"Nope." The lie slid easily off her tongue.

"Is Lauren doing well?"

Rachel didn't dare tell him the teen had hitched a ride into town with Satan's sidekick. "She's helping with the rodeos."

"Good. And Felix?"

"Felix is fine." She didn't mention that the black cat spent most of his day lying on the bench by the front door waiting for his master to return. Hoping to take her father's mind off home she asked, "Do you play cards?"

"I've been known to play a game of poker now and then."

Rachel dug through her purse and removed a deck of cards. "I'll teach you double solitaire." She scooted the desk chair closer to the bed. "Whoever wins buys dinner."

"Nothing I like better than a challenge."

They played cards for an hour and it took that long for Rachel to muster the courage to voice a question she'd been dying to ask for years. "Why didn't you come to my high-school graduation?"

Her father's gaze flew to her face. After a moment he set his cards aside. "I wanted to be there."

"What stopped you?"

P.T. stared into space. "I assumed you wouldn't want me there."

Throat aching, Rachel struggled to swallow. Her vision blurred and her chest tightened until she couldn't breathe. She left her father's bedside and stood before the window. "I wanted you there."

"I'm sorry, Rachel."

She'd gotten the apology she'd hoped for, but the words failed to erase years of hurt and pain.

"Your aunt sent your graduation announcement from the local newspaper and a picture of you in your gown, holding your diploma." His voice lowered to a whisper. "The framed photo is on my nightstand."

Funny how she'd believed P.T. hadn't cared about her when in reality he had. She studied her father's reflection in the window glass. He appeared frail, hardly the forbidding man she'd assumed he'd be. *What if he doesn't beat the cancer?*

Rachel shoved the thought aside. She didn't want to consider she might not have enough time to renew her relationship with her father.

Chapter Eight

"Folks, gate number three is where the final ride in the men's bronc-bustin' competition takes place. For those of you attendin' the thirty-fifth annual Canyon City Rodeo and Livestock Show for the first time, C. J. Rodriguez is a rising star in this event." Cheers echoed through the stands. "C.J. needs an 87 tonight to take first place. Let's see if his horse, Freckles, cooperates!"

The chute door opened and Freckles leaped for freedom. C.J. hung on tight, spurring high on the bronc's shoulders. When the gelding's front hooves hit the dirt, daylight shone between C.J.'s backside and the saddle. The cowboy and bronc engaged in a ballet of spins and bucks, testing each other's strength and stamina. Right as the buzzer sounded, C.J.'s hat flew off. He leaped from Freckles, landing on his feet. In dramatic fashion he swept his Stetson off the ground and bowed to the fans, triggering an ear-deafening round of boot stomping and applause.

"That was some mighty fine ridin' from C. J. Rodriguez!" the announcer hollered from his booth above the stands. "C.J. makes bronc bustin' look like a walk in the park. I gotta feeling that young man is headin' to the finals in Vegas later this year."

While the announcer recapped the men's winning rides, Rachel and Lauren stood in the cowboy-ready area with the female bull riders waiting for the women's event to kick off.

"Excuse me. Are you Rachel Lewis?"

Rachel twirled and came face-to-face with C. J. Rodriguez. The cowboy wasn't much taller than Rachel but his movie-star looks and cocky grin made him appear six feet tall. "I'm Rachel."

He tipped his hat. "Just wanted to thank you for bringing in these talented women—" he swept his hat toward the lady bull riders gathered behind Rachel, then winked at Lauren whose mouth hung open as she stared at C.J. "—to ride bulls. Haven't seen this much excitement at a small-town rodeo in a long time." He plopped his hat on his head. "Good luck today, ladies."

"Wow. He's hot," Lauren said, her gaze glued to C.J.'s backside as he strolled off.

"Was that C.J.?" Dixie Cash said, shoving a paper bag at Rachel. Dixie was the newest cowgirl Shannon had found to participate in the rodeo.

"Yep. He stopped to wish you ladies good luck today," Rachel said. "What's this?" She jiggled the bag.

"A sample of my homemade soaps."

Rachel opened the bag and sniffed. The scent of spice and flowers tickled a sneeze out of her.

"Bless you," Dixie said.

"They smell delicious." When Rachel learned Dixie made organic soaps and sold them in tourist shops, she'd insisted on buying several bars to take back to friends in Providence.

"Let me know which ones you like best and I'll put together a gift basket for you."

"That would be great, thanks, Dixie." The more Rachel learned about the women bull riders, the more they impressed her—not only with their courage but their ingenuity and talents outside of rodeo.

All the same, Rachel prayed the six rides would go off without a hitch. She'd lied to the stock contractor, insisting Clint had threatened to take Five Star Rodeos' business elsewhere if the man refused to bring additional bulls for the women at no extra charge. Clint had volunteered to be a bullfighter and Rachel was counting on high ticket sales to make up for the added expense of paying a second bullfighter to cover the event.

The announcer mentioned the mayor's name and Mitch McDonnell's chest puffed like a bullfrog. He waved to the crowd and flashed a big grin. He had no qualms about allowing the public to believe adding women's bull riding to the program had been his suggestion. What was it about men needing to be the brains behind every good idea?

She wondered if a bruised ego was the reason Clint had balked at setting up a practice pen for the women. As a matter of fact, her go-to man's reluctance to lend a helping hand puzzled Rachel. He acted as if he didn't want to her to succeed, which didn't make sense because he had as much at stake as she did in the summer rodeos.

"Ladies." Rachel spun at the sound of Clint's voice and gaped.

Dressed in long red athletic shorts, black socks that covered his knees, a red-and-yellow short-sleeved jersey and white shoes with cleats, Clint looked ridiculous.

"I viewed the bulls for today." Clint's mouth tightened. "There's one I don't like."

"Which bull?" Shannon asked.

"Hot Chocolate."

"That's mine," Julie Kenner said. The young woman had competed in barrel racing in high school and had attended a bronc-riding clinic for women a year ago. This afternoon would be Julie's first experience riding a bull.

"Hot Chocolate is bigger than all the rest," Clint said. "He's at least a twenty-point bull."

Julie rolled her shoulders. "Doesn't matter. I won't last eight seconds anyway."

A little piece of Rachel's heart broke off at the realization that Clint had taken the time to check out the bulls then warn Julie about hers—especially seeing how he didn't support a women's rough-stock event. "I don't want you getting hurt," Rachel said. "I'll ask the officials if they'll allow you to ride a different bull."

"I've already checked and they said Julie would have to scratch if she didn't ride Hot Chocolate," Clint said.

Blast it. The fans would not be pleased if Julie didn't compete. They'd paid to watch six women ride bulls, not five.

"I'll be fine," Julie said.

"If you're determined to ride Hot Chocolate, then here's what I want you to do." Clint stared the young woman in the eye. "The minute the bull clears the chute, release the rope and lean to your right. The bull's momentum will throw you. Once you hit the ground, I'll move between you and the bull while my partner distracts Hot Chocolate. Get to the rails as fast as you can."

"Got it." Julie tugged on her riding glove.

"Are you sure?" Rachel asked Julie.

"No worries." Julie joined her friends who'd gathered in a circle, heads bent, hands clasped. Rachel guessed they were saying a prayer and sent a silent request of her own toward heaven, asking the powers that be to keep each woman safe.

"I don't have a good feeling about today." Rachel inched closer to Clint. She caught a whiff of sandalwood cologne and decided he was the best-smelling thing she'd sniffed all day. Maybe the butterflies in her stomach warning of impending danger were meant for her and not the lady bull riders.

"Randy and I will keep everyone safe." Clint stared at the VIP section. "Mitch McDonnell appears happy with the turnout."

After putting up a stink earlier in the week about constructing the makeshift practice pen for the women, Rachel was pleased that Clint wanted to converse with her. "Let's hope word about our women's rough-stock event spreads and we sell out next month's rodeo."

"Shannon's radio interview was a big hit," Clint said.

"Lauren gets credit for that coup. She phoned

the station and told them that you suggested they put Shannon on the air."

"I'm relieved my daughter's found something to take her mind off how miserable she's been this summer."

"Me, too." Rachel hadn't heard the teen utter a word about being bored or tired of the ranch since she'd become her assistant.

"Ladies and gents...get ready for the first-ever Canyon City Rodeo women's bull-riding event!"

"Showtime," Clint said.

Rachel reached for Clint's arm but he stepped away and her fingers brushed his hand. "Be careful."

"Will do." He strolled off.

"Our first female contender is Skylar Riggins. She's a twenty-three-year-old medical transcriptionist from Yuma, who claims she can tame any bull, whether he's got two legs or four." The announcer snickered at the lame joke. "Skylar's gonna strut her stuff on Mr. Loco."

Rachel watched Skylar adjust her headgear while Shannon tightened the straps on her friend's protective vest. The face mask over the helmet made it impossible for Rachel to read Skylar's expression as she settled gingerly on Mr. Loco's back. Skylar wrapped the bull rope around her right hand then signaled to the gateman. The chute door swung open and Mr. Loco went to work.

The bull was strong but Skylar hung on tight, her slim body jerking with each buck. As the seconds ticked off, Clint moved closer to the bull, should Skylar get tossed. His partner, Randy, waved his arms attempting to gain the bull's attention.

Rachel switched her gaze to Skylar just as she sailed through the air. The buzzer sounded a moment later. Clint rushed forward, positioning his body between Skylar and Mr. Loco. Randy approached from the other side and grabbed the bull rope which distracted Mr. Loco long enough for Skylar to climb to her feet and run for the rails. Once the bull realized his rider had vanished, he trotted off to the bull pen on his own.

"Looks like Mr. Loco got the best of Ms. Riggins. Better luck next time, missy!"

Wendy rode second and hit the dirt as soon as her bull cleared the chute. Kim was third but got thrown at the five-second mark. Dixie, the youngest of the women at twenty-three, kept her seat for six seconds.

"We're down to two cowgirls, folks. Let's see if Julie Kenner, who's another Yuma gal, can tame Hot Chocolate, a bull famous for bein' feisty."

Julie scaled the chute rails and plopped onto the back of the bull. Rachel squeezed her hands into fists so tightly her knuckles ached. The chute door opened and Hot Chocolate went to work. The first buck almost unseated Julie. Rachel waited for the young woman to release the bull rope as Clint had instructed her to do, but Julie held on. The bull twisted right, left, then right in quick succession and Julie slid sideways.

A collective gasp rippled through the crowd when Julie hung upside down along the bull's side, her head dangerously close to the animal's back hooves. Hot Chocolate spun toward the chute and Rachel prayed the bull wouldn't slam Julie against the metal rails. The buzzer sounded and the crowd went wild. Julie struggled to regain her balance but instead slipped further beneath the bull. If Julie released the rope now, she'd fall beneath the bull's belly and get stomped.

Risking his own safety, Clint rushed to Julie's side. Once he freed her hand from the rigging, he tugged Julie off Hot Chocolate. He dragged her by the arm away from the bull's vicious kicks, then released her next to the rails before helping Randy distract the bull.

"Are you all right?" Rachel rushed to Julie's side.

"I might have dislocated my shoulder." Julie

cradled her arm against her chest, her face tight with pain.

"Lauren, you and Wendy take Julie to the first-aid station. I'll be there as soon as Shannon finishes her ride."

"Julie scored a seventy-eight! Not bad for hangin' upside down most of her ride. We got one more cowgirl ready to strut her stuff. Shannon Douglas from Stagecoach, Arizona, is about to tame Sweet Sassafras!"

While Shannon settled on the bull, Clint and Randy stood on either side of the gate ready to leap into action. Rachel imagined how tired Clint must be with little time to catch his breath between each ride.

"Shannon's no stranger to bulls. She's competed in rough-stock events since she graduated from high school and was named rookie of the year in 2010." The JumboTron displayed a picture of fireworks as music blared through the stands. "Let's see if Shannon can make it to eight!"

One more twist of the bull rope and Shannon nodded to the gateman. Sweet Sassafras spun Shannon in a circle then performed a series of bucks but was unable to toss her from his back. Rachel stared at the seconds ticking off the JumboTron.

C'mon, Shannon. You can do it.

The buzzer rang and the crowd went ballistic. "That was some ride by Shannon Douglas!"

Shannon waited for the right moment and launched herself off the bull. She landed on her feet, stumbled once then ran for the rails. Sweet Sassafras ignored Shannon and allowed Randy to guide him from the arena.

"Shannon Douglas earned an 84—good enough for first place!"

As soon as Shannon's boots hit the dirt in the cowboy-ready area, Rachel hugged her. "You were fabulous!"

The cowgirl removed her headgear and gasped. "How's Julie?"

"I'm on my way to find out. Grab your gear and meet me at the first-aid station." Rachel weaved through the crowd toward the EMS truck parked near the livestock pens. She poked her head inside the vehicle. Julie's arm rested in a sling and a paramedic held an ice pack against her shoulder. "How's the patient?" she asked.

"Dislocated her shoulder but I put it back in place," the paramedic said. "I suggested she make an appointment with her personal physician to determine if she needs an MRI. She might have torn a ligament."

"I'm sorry, Rachel," Julie said.

"You have nothing to be sorry for. I hope

your shoulder heals quickly and doesn't keep you out of work."

"I've got a few vacation days if I need them." Julie shifted on the cot, wincing when she jostled her injured arm. "Do you think Shannon will find a replacement for me before the Boot Hill Rodeo?"

"She will. Don't worry."

A moment later Shannon pulled Rachel aside. "I'll try to find another girl to take Julie's spot but I can't guarantee I'll find one in time."

"I'll ride," Lauren said, joining the conversation.

"Your father said no bull riding, remember?" Rachel said.

"I've watched the others all week and I've practiced on the mechanical bull in the barn. I can do it."

"A machine is different from a real bull," Rachel said.

"Then, let me practice on real bulls." Lauren refused to drop the subject.

"I've been riding bulls for a few years and I get thrown more than I stay on," Shannon said.

Convinced Clint wouldn't allow his daughter to get anywhere near a bull, Rachel said, "You'll have to get your father's permission first."

Wendy, Skylar and Kim arrived. "Where's Dixie?" Rachel asked.

Shannon glanced over her shoulder. Dixie stood a few yards away chatting with a handsome cowboy. "Hey, Dix! You coming with us or not?"

Dixie waved them off.

"Where's the party?" Julie stepped outside the EMS truck. "Drinks are on me." She giggled.

"The paramedic gave her a shot for pain," Wendy said. "She's as high as a kite."

"We're signing a few autographs for the kids then heading over to Bubba Tubs Barbecue to celebrate." Kim looked at Lauren. "You're welcome to come along."

"You don't need my help, do you?" Lauren asked Rachel.

The teen had worked hard preparing for the rodeo and deserved to have fun. "Can you drop Lauren off at the entrance to the fairground by eleven o'clock tonight?"

"Sure," Kim said.

"Thanks, Rachel." Lauren beamed.

"No drinking," Rachel warned.

"We'll order Lauren Shirley Temples," Wendy joked.

"I'm serious." The last thing Rachel needed was Clint blaming her for encouraging his underage daughter to drink.

Shannon slung an arm over Lauren's shoulder. "We've got her back."

Deciding Lauren was in good hands, Rachel went searching for Clint. She found him guzzling a water bottle near the bull pen.

"That was some ride by Shannon," she said, announcing her presence.

"If she can avoid injury and find a few more rodeos to compete in throughout the year, she'll be as good as any cowboy on the circuit." Clint tossed the plastic water bottle into a garbage can. "How's Julie?"

"Dislocated shoulder."

"Damn." He shook his head. "I shouldn't have grabbed her arm like I did."

"You didn't have a choice. You had to drag her to safety or she'd have been trampled by the bull."

"You're down to five riders."

"'Fraid so. Shannon's going to look for a replacement." She considered telling Clint that Lauren had volunteered but decided that fight was best left between father and daughter. "After the girls sign autographs, they're going out for barbecue. They invited Lauren along but promised to bring her back to the rodeo grounds by eleven tonight."

"We'll have a couple of hours to kill after we tie up the loose ends here."

Exactly what Rachel had been thinking. "We could grab a bite to eat." Her pulse quickened when Clint's gaze dropped to her chest before returning to her face.

"A steak dinner sounds good," he said.

"I've got a media interview in a few minutes."

"Okay. I'll change clothes then help load the animals in the livestock trailers. I'll meet you at the cashier's booth when I finish."

"See you in a little while." She turned to leave but Clint's voice stopped her.

"Rachel."

Her name left his mouth in a whisper. "Yes?"

"I'm looking forward to dinner."

"Me, too." Rachel hurried away before she did something stupid like tell Clint she thought he looked sexy in knee socks.

"THANKS FOR YOUR HELP." Steve Gentry shut the door after the last bull had been loaded into the livestock trailer.

"We need to talk," Clint said.

Steve glanced at his watch. "I've got to be in Oklahoma next weekend for a rodeo and these bulls need to rest a few days before another road trip. The sooner I put them to pasture the better." He stepped toward the driver's door but Clint blocked his path.

"Hot Chocolate has no business in a women's rough-stock event," Clint said.

"I did you a favor by bringing in extra bulls."

"Julie Kenner could have been trampled to death if she'd fallen beneath that bull."

"Look," Gentry said. "I scrambled like hell to find lesser-point bulls for the women. Hot Chocolate didn't work out. Big deal. No harm done."

"Don't use that bull in the Boot Hill Rodeo."

Gentry scoffed. "Or what?"

"Five Star Rodeos will find another stock contractor." There were other contractors in the business who'd be happy to add Five Star Rodeos to their client list, but P.T. and Gentry went back a long way and Clint hoped Gentry would cooperate. Clint didn't want to explain to P.T. why a longtime business association had been severed.

"I'll find a replacement for the bull," Gentry grumbled.

"Appreciate that." Clint tipped his hat and weaved through the livestock pens. Satisfied no animals had been left behind, he made his way across the rodeo grounds to the cashier's booth. When he arrived at the front office, Rachel was engaged in conversation with Mayor McDonnell.

"Clint." McDonnell flashed a big grin. "Hell

of a show those gals put on tonight. P.T. should have had you running the rodeos years ago."

"I told you the rodeo would be in good hands with Clint in charge." Rachel batted her eyelashes at the mayor.

"Hope you'll spread the word on how satisfied you were with the women's rough-stock event."

"Be happy to sing your praises." McDonnell walked off, leaving Clint alone with Rachel. He braced himself for an "I-told-you-so" but one never came.

"I'm hungry," Rachel said.

"Me, too." Instead of leading the way to his truck he studied Rachel, liking the way her snug jeans gloved her fanny. And the way the pearl snaps on her Western shirt sparkled beneath the fluorescent lights. His gaze dropped to the ground. "Nice boots. New?"

"I bought them this morning at the Justin booth."

"You're turning into a regular cowgirl."

Rachel laughed. "Not a chance."

"There's a restaurant five miles from here that serves a mean steak." He led the way outside but stopped when he recalled Rachel's comment about not eating red meat. "The place only serves steak. If you want we can try a different restaurant."

"No, that's fine. I haven't had a steak in months."

By the time they pulled into the parking lot of the Pack Mule, Clint's jeans had become uncomfortably tight, suggesting he'd rather be doing something other than eating with Rachel.

"Looks like a popular place," she said.

"It's not fancy, but they serve cowboy-size portions."

Once inside, the hostess showed them to a table. As they walked through the restaurant several patrons waved to Clint or called his name. Most were old cronies of P.T.'s. A waitress named Ellen arrived with a basket of fresh-baked bread and honey-flavored butter. "What can I get you folks to drink?"

"I'll have a glass of your house wine," Rachel said.

"Water'll do for me," Clint said.

"Need a few more minutes or are you ready to order?" Ellen asked.

"Is there a menu I can see?" Rachel frowned.

"We serve steak, steak and steak. No chicken. No fish. Just steak."

"I'll take the porterhouse cut, rare." Clint spoke to Rachel. "They offer a lady's filet mignon."

"Sure," Rachel said. "Medium well, please."

"Baked potato or steak fries?" Ellen asked.

"Baked potato."

"Me, too," Clint said. "Loaded."

The waitress glanced at Rachel.

"Loaded, also."

"Be back in a jiffy."

After Ellen left, Clint asked, "Tired?"

"I'm bushed and I wasn't the one busting bulls or rescuing cowgirls."

"I think the fans were surprised at how competitive the women were."

"Mayor Larsen and Mayor Ross interviewed the vendors at the rodeo throughout the day and were pleased with the positive responses from the merchants."

Go on. Tell her. "I owe you an apology. I thought for sure your idea to bring in a women's rough-stock event would fail to increase attendance."

"I took a chance and it paid off."

Rachel had the right to gloat but she didn't and Clint's admiration for her upped a notch. "The rodeo in Boot Hill is four weeks away and we're one bull rider short."

"Shannon will find someone." Rachel's voice rang with confidence.

Clint wasn't convinced Shannon would find a replacement for Julie. Women bull riders were few and far between. If another rider couldn't be found the event would be canceled, putting the success of the rodeo at risk.

Well, it's not my problem. Clint knew of a couple women in the area who might consider filling Julie's spot, but why help Rachel look good in P.T.'s eyes? Oh, hell, he was damned confused about everything—his relationship with P.T., Rachel's relationship with her father. The more he learned about Rachel the more he sympathized with the position P.T. had put her in this summer. As far as Clint was concerned, the whole situation was a sticky mess none of them could easily wash their hands of.

Ellen delivered their meals and he watched Rachel scrape half the cheese and sour cream off her potato before taking a bite.

"You're a health nut, aren't you?"

She smiled. "The older I become the more difficult it is to keep off the pounds."

"I don't know why you're worried. You have a great body."

Her face flushed at his compliment. "I work hard to stay in shape." She waved her fork in the air. "I have to walk the talk in front of the student athletes."

Clint didn't want to discuss Rachel's job. He was more interested in her personal life. "Are you in a relationship right now?"

If his direct question bothered her she didn't

show it. "I was engaged once, but it didn't work out."

P.T. never mentioned an engagement, but then again he might not have known. "The guy's a jerk," Clint said.

"How do you mean?"

"For cheating on you."

Rachel's eyes widened.

"When someone says *it didn't work out* that means one of them cheated." He narrowed his gaze. "You weren't the cheater."

"Thank you...I think." Rachel finished her wine in two swallows. "Mike was in Japan on a business trip when he met another woman. He married her overseas then returned to the States, broke the news to me and cleared his things out of my condo before leaving the country." Rachel smiled. "Your turn."

"I proposed to Lauren's mother when she learned she was pregnant, but Liz didn't want to marry a cowboy. She wanted a man who worked nine to five and whose job came with health insurance, benefits and a fat wallet."

"Did Liz find that man?"

"Too soon to tell if husband number five is him." Clint gave in to the need to know more about Rachel's private life. "Back to you," he said. "Are you dating anyone in Rhode Island?"

He figured men of all ages would stand in line for a chance with a woman like Rachel.

"Nope." She smiled. "I tried online dating but that was a disaster."

"Don't leave me hanging." He chuckled. "What happened?"

"None of my dates resembled their profile pictures."

"How many dates did you go on?"

"Six before I shut down my account."

Ellen appeared, setting a second glass of wine on the table and refilling Clint's water glass. "How does everything taste?"

"Delicious," Rachel said. Then continued after Ellen left again. "Five of the men pushed for sex on the first date to see if we were compatible. The sixth guy claimed he was a born-again virgin and wouldn't have sex until we were officially engaged."

Clint couldn't contain his need to know if Rachel had slept with her dates. "Did you have sex with any of them?"

"Of course not."

He loved the way her pale skin flushed pink when she was embarrassed.

"What about you?" she asked.

"I broke up several months ago with a woman I'd had an on-again off-again relationship with for several years. Monica finally accepted that

I wasn't going to propose so she ran off with a salesman from Vegas nine months ago."

Country Western music filtered through the wall of the restaurant, affording Clint a reason to change the subject. "There's a live band playing next door. We've got time for a dance or two before we meet Lauren at the fairgrounds."

"I don't know any of those fancy line dances."

"Me, neither." Clint stood and offered his hand. Rachel placed her fingers in his and he swore his body temperature spiked ten degrees. "I'll show you the kind of dancing I know best."

"Oh? What kind is that?"

"The kind where we hold each other close and sway."

Chapter Nine

A live band played a George Strait ballad as Clint pressed his palm against Rachel's lower back and guided her toward the corner of the crowded dance floor. The warmth of his touch felt right—not awkward, as Rachel had feared. Holding her left hand prisoner against his chest, they swayed…his hips gliding right then left, bumping softly against her thighs.

The easy rhythm lulled Rachel closer… closer…until her breasts brushed his chest. Was it her imagination or had his hold tightened?

This isn't smart, Rachel.

Two weeks had passed since she'd arrived in Stagecoach and Clint was far from being a stranger. Her physical attraction to him was no surprise—what woman wouldn't find the handsome cowboy sexy? But there was more to Clint than male magnetism, and the sparks flying between them weren't all sexual. They were both stubborn and had a tendency to dig their heels in before hearing all the facts. Their face-offs created a palpable energy in the air that invigorated Rachel and fed into her determination to conquer any challenge thrown her way.

Don't be melodramatic. Your hormones are in overdrive.

Granted, she hadn't had sex since her breakup with Mike, making her hyperaware of Clint's sexual magnetism.

On a cerebral level, Rachel struggled with Clint's loyalty to her father. She understood what spawned his devotion—P.T. had provided Clint with a stable home and made him feel valued and wanted after a tough childhood in foster care. She didn't begrudge Clint his happy-ever-after, but his close relationship with P.T. made it more difficult for Rachel to reconnect with her father.

"You're frowning," Clint whispered in her ear. "What's going through that pretty head of yours?"

She leaned back and stared. Clint's Stetson cast a shadow over his face, hiding his eyes from view. Dare she tell the truth—that the little girl inside her was jealous of his bond with her father? That she was angry at P.T. for casting her aside then later taking in Clint?

Deciding to hold her tongue, Rachel said,

"Tomorrow's Sunday. Let's visit my father. Maybe Lauren would like to come along, too."

"P.T. doesn't want visitors."

"My father's bluffing. He appreciated my company a few days ago."

Clint tucked Rachel against him in a way that left no doubt she excited him. "Okay," he whispered, his lips grazing her ear.

Okay, what? Was Clint asking her permission to touch her or was he agreeing to accompany her to Phoenix? Before she found her voice he took her by the hand and led her through a side door, which opened onto an alley alongside the building. Once the door closed behind them, he pinned her against the brick building.

"I want to kiss you."

Rachel had less than a second to process Clint's statement before his mouth covered hers. His lips teased and toyed, drugging her with their velvety touch. When he ended the kiss Rachel moaned.

"More?"

"Yes." She wasn't sure if she spoke the word or if Clint read her mind. He made love to her mouth, his lips and tongue creating a deep ache in her stomach that spread through her limbs. Fearing her legs would collapse, she wrapped her arms around his neck.

He flicked his tongue over her lips then entered her mouth in a slow, sensual glide. Good Lord, the man was a wicked kisser. One more sweep of his tongue inside her mouth, then he pulled away and rested his cheek against hers. Neither spoke, their ragged breathing a testament to the heat of their kiss. Clint's warm male scent enveloped Rachel, making her feel safe, comforted, desired. Her fingers tightened against his neck, reluctant to release him.

Clint cleared his throat, ending the magical moment. "Go ahead," he muttered.

"Go ahead what?"

"Curse me. Punch me."

"Why?"

"For taking that kiss too far."

He regretted kissing her? "You didn't want to?"

"Hell, yes, I wanted to kiss you." He paced several steps away.

"Then why are you upset?"

"We shouldn't…" He stared at the ground.

Terrific. She'd experienced the sexiest, most erotic kiss of her life and now the guy regretted it. Straightening her shirt she attempted to step past him.

Clint grasped her hand. "It's not that I didn't enjoy kissing you…it's that—"

"It was a kiss." She yanked her hand away. "No big deal."

He glanced at his watch. "We'd better head to the rodeo grounds to meet Lauren."

They drove in silence, Rachel replaying their kiss in her head. As much as Clint turned her on, he was smart to invoke the no-more-crossing-the-line rule. Becoming intimate with her father's foreman would only muddle her mission.

"I SAID NO VISITORS. What does an old man have to do to get people to listen to him?" P.T. grumbled after Clint entered his hospital room.

"I'll leave if you're not in the mood for company."

"Be rude of me to send you home after you drove all this way." The sparkle in P.T.'s eyes betrayed his grouchy demeanor.

Clint crossed the room and stared out the window. "Nice view." He settled into the recliner and extended the leg rest.

"My doctor wants me to sit outside more often."

"Why's that?"

"I'm guessing he believes if I surround myself with living things I won't notice I'm dying."

P.T.'s morose words caught Clint by surprise. Until now, P.T. had maintained a positive attitude about his condition. "Has your cancer spread?"

"No."

"Then what's bugging you?"

"I miss working the rodeos." P.T. gestured toward the door. "Did Rachel and Lauren come with you?"

"I dropped the girls off at the mall. When they finish shopping they'll catch a cab and head over here."

"Don't keep me in suspense. How'd the Canyon City Rodeo turn out?"

Clint hoped P.T.'s cronies hadn't informed him that Rachel had added a women's roughstock event to the schedule. "You talk to any of your friends?"

"I phoned Mitch McDonnell but he hasn't returned my call."

"The mayor's too busy preening. The rodeo broke last year's attendance records."

P.T. sat up straighter. "You don't say? Did Gentry bring in better bucking stock this year?"

Go with it. "He did and C. J. Rodriguez won both the bull and the saddle bronc competitions."

"That youngun' might go all the way this year." P.T. rubbed his hand down his whiskered cheek. "I had my doubts about asking Rachel to help this summer, but it looks like I worried for nothing." He stared thoughtfully. "How are you and Rachel getting along?"

Too well for our own good. "Lauren's helping Rachel with the rodeos."

"Got to keep teenagers busy or they'll get into trouble."

"I don't remember giving you any problems."

"Once you decided to bust bulls you were too tired to misbehave." P.T. shook his head. "I was against you riding bulls, but I guess you knew that."

No, Clint had not known P.T.'s feelings about the sport. "You never told me you disapproved."

"You were eighteen."

"Why didn't you speak your mind?" Clint pressed.

"Wasn't my place to tell you what you could or couldn't do. You weren't rightfully my son."

Clint's lungs seized up on him, making breathing difficult. P.T. had treated him like a son but deep down hadn't considered Clint his child. The moment P.T. had become his foster parent Clint had believed they'd become a family—the two of them. Even when he'd learned of Rachel's existence, he hadn't felt threatened because she lived far away and had little contact with her father. He didn't want to accept that P.T. put Rachel ahead of him.

Maybe you were never number one.

The thought sent a sharp pain through Clint's chest.

"That first year you rode the circuit I said a prayer when you climbed on the back of each bull," P.T. said.

"You weren't the only one praying." Clint braved a smile. He might not have been P.T.'s son but at least the old man had cared enough to be concerned about him. P.T. stared into space, his brow furrowed.

"What's troubling you?" Clint asked.

"When a man hears the word *cancer* he recalls all the mistakes he made in his life and worries he won't have time to square things with the people he wronged."

"You never wronged me. I'm grateful to you for giving me a home," Clint said.

"You wouldn't be thankful if you knew the real reason I took you in."

Stunned, Clint opened his mouth to ask P.T. to explain, but a knock on the door interrupted them.

"You awake, P.T.?" Lauren popped her head into the room.

"I've got cancer, not narcolepsy."

Lauren went straight to P.T. and hugged him. "Did you finish *Planet Destiny?*"

"Read the final chapter last night. Can't figure out what you young girls find so fascinating about a young man with hair down to his knees and skin as red as a lobster tail."

Lauren laughed. "Yeah, Zordan's hot, isn't he?"

"Zordan was a fool to take on the Androids by himself."

"He had to defeat their army in order to free Princess Miriam from the clutches of evil Lord Trent."

"Miriam should have never fallen for Lord Trent's false promises," P.T. argued.

"Girls will do anything for love."

Clint wondered if Rachel had answered P.T.'s call for help not because he was her father and in poor health but because she, too, yearned for love? "Where's Rachel?" Clint asked.

"She stopped in the gift shop."

"Have you read any of the Zane Gray novels?" P.T. spoke to Lauren.

"I'm halfway through *Riders of the Purple Sage.*"

"What do you think?"

"I like that Jane Withersteen owns her own ranch and I don't blame her for not wanting to marry some old man in their church, but the writing is lame."

"That book was written in 1912. Back then, people—" He stopped talking when Rachel entered the room.

"Sorry if I'm interrupting." Rachel set a shopping bag by the door and smiled at her father. "How are you feeling?"

"I'm still here," P.T. groused.

"Lauren, what do you say we check out the cafeteria while Rachel visits with P.T.?"

"You don't have to leave," Rachel protested, but Clint and Lauren waltzed out of the room, shutting the door behind them. Left alone with her father, she retreated to the window. "The terrace sure is a popular place." Eleven patients visited with friends and family.

"Clint said the Canyon City Rodeo broke attendance records."

"Mayor McDonnell was pleased." She eyed her father's reflection in the glass.

"I hear Lauren's helping you. What do you have her doing?"

"Answering the phone, sending out flyers." Rachel didn't care to discuss the rodeos. She sat in the recliner, aware of her father's eyes on her. The air in the room thickened with tension. Why was it so difficult to speak about the past?

"Are you going to ask me or just sit there?" he said.

"Ask you what?"

"Why I sent you to live with my sister."

They were going to have the come-to-Jesus talk right now—with Lauren and Clint returning any minute? "I am curious as to why you took Clint in but couldn't see fit to raise your own daughter."

P.T. dropped his gaze to his lap.

"Don't get me wrong," Rachel said. "What you did for Clint was generous and noble, but I'm suspicious of why you suddenly needed my help this summer after wanting nothing to do with me most of my life."

A sigh escaped P.T. "I believed I was acting in your best interest by sending you to live with my sister."

"I was five years old. I'd lost my mother. How could you think I'd be better off without both my parents?"

"Because the only parent you had left didn't trust himself to keep you safe from harm if you remained on the ranch."

"I don't understand. Why would you believe something bad would happen to me if I lived with you?"

The answer to Rachel's question would have to wait when the door opened and Clint came back into the room, Lauren on his heels.

"This is a really cool hospital, P.T. I like the game room." Lauren's gaze swung to Rachel. "There's an old-fashioned pinball machine and an air-hockey table next to the cafeteria."

"Nothing but the best, kiddo." P.T.'s smile failed to hide the pain in his eyes when he looked at Rachel.

"We should head back to Stagecoach," Rachel said.

"Wait a second." P.T. rummaged through the drawer in the nightstand next to his bed. "With everything going on I'd forgotten that I'd booked a houseboat on Lake Powell last year for the July Fourth holiday." He held up a white envelope. "I'd planned to invite a few business associates to discuss the possibility of expanding Five Star Rodeos' summer schedule, but with me stuck here, the men have made other plans. Too late for a refund and it'd be a shame to waste those days on the boat. You three go in my place?"

Was her father trying to make amends for the proverbial bomb he'd dropped on her a few minutes ago? No matter his objective, Rachel conceded that she would enjoy a break from the ranch. "I'd love to see more of Arizona," she said. Now that the groundwork had been laid with the media, and interviews scheduled for the Boot Hill Rodeo July 16th and 17th, there was little else to do.

"We're right in the middle of a busy rodeo season," Clint said.

He acted as if being stuck with Rachel on a boat in the middle of a lake would be torture… unless he considered being alone with her torture of a sensual kind.

P.T. handed Rachel the envelope. "The marina number's in there. Call and tell them you're taking my place."

Rachel offered a token of resistance. "Like Clint said, Dad, we're busy preparing for the next rodeo. We don't have time—"

"A few days won't make or break any rodeo schedule." P.T. pointed at Clint. "Ask Mark Donner to feed the stock and watch the ranch while you're gone. He owes me for taking in that renegade bull that attacked his herd."

Rachel shrugged and mouthed the word *whatever* when Clint looked at her.

"Stay well." Clint patted P.T.'s shoulder.

Lauren hugged P.T. "I miss you."

Torn over needing her father's hug and wanting to run from the room, Rachel took a step toward the bed, but chickened out at the last second. "Take care of yourself." She left the room first and waited in the hall for Lauren and Clint.

The drive back to Stagecoach took forever. Lauren listened to her iPod. Clint fiddled with the radio every half hour. Rachel stared out the window.

When Clint pulled into the ranch yard, he said, "We didn't stop for supper on the way home. I could throw a few hamburgers on the grill."

"Thanks, but I'm not hungry." Rachel hopped out of the truck and shut the door in his face.

"Dad?"

"Yeah?"

"Rachel didn't even hug P.T. goodbye."

"You noticed, huh?"

"Is she mad at him?"

"Why would you think that?"

"I thought maybe Rachel was upset because he got sick. I know it doesn't make sense but my sociology teacher said when people feel helpless they become angry. Rachel probably wishes she could cure P.T.'s cancer."

"I suppose."

"You should go talk to her, Dad. Tell her P.T.'s cancer isn't her fault."

"I think Rachel needs her space." He got out of the truck and walked with Lauren to the cabin.

"Dad?"

"What?"

"Shannon and her friends are coming over tomorrow afternoon."

"Okay." Clint was getting damned tired of corralling practice bulls, but he couldn't very well tell the women to find a new facility—not when they were the reason Five Star Rodeos kicked butt in Canyon City.

"I've been practicing on the mechanical bull

in the barn and I'm getting better. Shannon's been helping me. She thinks I'm ready to try a real bull."

"The hell you say!" Clint hadn't meant to yell, but he was so confused about his feelings for Rachel that he couldn't think straight. "Sorry." He exhaled slowly. "What level?" There were three levels on the bucking machine—beginner, intermediate and advanced.

"Beginner, but if I could practice on a real bull…" The yearning on his daughter's face tugged at Clint. He'd experienced that same desire when he'd asked P.T. to let him ride bulls.

"Please, Dad."

"You've never even ridden a horse," Clint said.

"I don't care about horses. I want to ride bulls."

"It's late." Clint wasn't in the mood for another go-round with his stubborn daughter. "We'll discuss this later."

"We never discuss. I ask. You say no." Lauren stomped off, but paused on the cabin steps. "Just when I was kinda of getting to like it here, you go and ruin it for me."

Lauren liked being here? Clint's resolve wavered. "Your mother would have a fit if she found out," he said.

"You'd be there watching me."

Damn straight he would. "Riding a bull isn't like other sports. There's balance and technique involved and you need to be able to judge the bull's next move."

"Then teach me. You were a bull rider." Lauren's eyes shone with hope. "Maybe I inherited your cowboy genes."

Giving his daughter pointers on bull riding would allow them to share a common interest and maybe by the grace of God help strengthen their relationship. He pointed a finger. "You only ride when I'm present."

"Promise."

"I mean it, Lauren. If I discover you've ridden a bull behind my back, you're done."

"Understood." Lauren clapped her hands together.

"And don't tell your mom."

"It'll be our secret."

Another secret. There seemed to be a lot of secrets floating around Five Star Ranch these days.

Chapter Ten

"Are you sure about this, Lauren?" Clint watched his daughter settle onto Curly's back. Before he'd escorted the bull into the bucking pen, he'd had a long chat with Curly, reminding the retired rodeo rock star that if not for P.T. granting him sanctuary at the ranch, his hide would be covering a rich man's floor.

"I can do this." Lauren's mouth pursed with determination but her confident demeanor did little to reassure Clint.

Not an hour went by that he didn't regret agreeing to teach his daughter the finer points of bull riding, but working together had brought about an uneasy peace between them and Clint was reluctant for their relationship to return to sullen teen vs. bewildered father.

"Hold the bull rope with both hands," he said.

"I'm ready for one hand," she insisted.

"Squeeze your—"

"You've told me this stuff a million times."

Lauren glanced across the corral. "Rachel's coming."

Clint braced himself. He'd kept his contact with Rachel to a minimum since their visit with P.T. in Phoenix. While she promoted the Boot Hill Rodeo, he spent his days feeding livestock and babysitting Lauren in the bull pen. Nights were a different story. As soon as his head hit the pillow, thoughts and images of Rachel crowded his mind. Their kiss the night of the Canyon City Rodeo had changed everything between them. He no longer associated Rachel with being P.T.'s daughter. Instead, he viewed her as a sexy, feisty, desirable woman— a woman he wanted in his bed.

"Another lesson?" Rachel stopped next to the chute.

"Dad says I still have to hang on with both hands."

"Is she ready, Clint?" Rachel asked.

He liked the way Rachel's blond hair shone almost white beneath the hot afternoon sun. "She's ready," he muttered. *But I'm not.*

"Make it to eight." Rachel high-fived Lauren.

"Get the gate, Dad." Lauren tightened the strap beneath her protective headgear.

Clenching his jaw, Clint opened the chute door and Curly leaped into action. The bull's twists and bucks lacked the vigor of the animals used in the Canyon City Rodeo, but Lauren had to fight hard to keep her seat.

After a moment Clint's adrenaline shoved aside his fear and he shouted, "Arm in the air!"

Lauren's arm shot high above her head, then Curly decided to be a stinker, kicking his back legs out and rolling his wide girth to the side. Lauren sailed through the air. She hit the ground but bounced to her feet before Curly figured out he no longer had a rider on his back and ceased bucking.

Brushing the dust from her jeans, Lauren grinned. "How many seconds?"

"Six." His daughter might make it to eight before she returned to California at the end of the summer.

"Wait until I tell the girls when they show up to practice tomorrow." Lauren climbed out of the corral. "Shannon's gonna be surprised."

"You'll have to phone Shannon instead, because you won't be here," Rachel said.

"I won't?" Lauren glanced between Clint and Rachel.

"It's the July Fourth weekend. We're staying on the houseboat at the Wahweap Marina on Lake Powell."

Clint had hoped P.T. would forget about the houseboat. If the old man knew how badly Clint yearned for Rachel, he'd have never suggested the trip. The last thing Clint wanted to do was fight his attraction to Rachel in the close confines of a boat with no avenue of escape, save for drowning.

"Can I stay here?" Lauren asked. "I want to watch Shannon and the others practice."

"If you don't go, you'll disappoint P.T." And Clint didn't trust Lauren not to ride bulls while he was gone.

"What about the press?" Lauren asked.

"I've got everything under control," Rachel said. "I spoke with Mayor Ross and he confirmed that the billboard *Clint* suggested advertising women's bull riding went up outside the town limits of Boot Hill late last week."

"Cool." Lauren grinned. "Whose picture's on it?"

"A newspaper reporter sent in a photo of Shannon riding in the Canyon City Rodeo."

This was the first Clint had heard of a billboard. "How much did all this cost?"

"Mayor Ross paid for the advertisement," Rachel said. "He claims he'll be reimbursed in votes when his reelection campaign kicks off next year."

"Please, let me stay," Lauren begged.

"I don't like the idea of you being alone at the ranch," Clint said.

"Lauren can have the keys to my car in case

she needs to drive into town for anything," Rachel offered.

Clint wished Mel would have kept the Prius another week, but the mechanic had delivered the car yesterday, apologizing to Rachel for the delay in pounding out the dents in the hood. Rachel had accepted Mel's apology but only after he'd agreed to remove the nuisance charge from the final bill.

"What if Shannon and the others stay at the ranch this weekend with me?" Lauren glanced at Rachel. "Is it okay if they use the guest bedrooms?"

"Sure."

Feeling ganged up on by the two females, Clint gave in. "You can stay, Lauren, but you're only allowed to practice on Curly. No other bulls."

"I'm okay with that."

"I want a text message from you right before you ride and as soon as you get thrown."

Lauren crinkled her nose. "What if I make it to eight?"

"Then I want a phone call, not a text."

"Deal," Lauren said.

"How long will it take to drive to Lake Powell?" Rachel asked.

"About seven hours," Clint said.

"We should plan to leave before daybreak.

Guess I'd better pack." Rachel strolled away and Clint groaned.

"What's the matter, Dad? Don't you want to go with Rachel?"

Yes. No. He wanted to be with Rachel but every minute in her presence chipped away at his self-control.

"You like Rachel and I know she likes you," Lauren said.

If Clint hadn't succeeded in hiding his confusing feelings for Rachel from his daughter, then he wondered if P.T. had guessed something was going on between him and Rachel. *Nah.* If the old man had, he wouldn't have suggested the houseboat. "My personal life isn't any of your—"

"Business? C'mon, Dad. I'm eighteen. I know all about sex."

Clint hadn't asked his daughter if she was sexually active—he didn't want to know. As far as he was concerned, that was an issue better dealt with between mother and daughter.

"You never married Mom but that doesn't mean you've lived like a monk."

Clint wasn't used to sharing his feelings with his daughter, but if he wished for a more meaningful, deeper relationship with Lauren then he had to open up. "I haven't had many relationships through the years."

"I know. You never brought a woman with you when you came to visit. Never mentioned another woman when we talked on the phone. Never—"

"Okay, you get the idea that your old man is no Casanova." He chuckled, then sobered. "I like Rachel but she's got a life out east and my life is here. Besides, she's P.T.'s daughter."

"What does being P.T.'s daughter have to do with liking Rachel?"

Everything. "P.T. wants the best for Rachel." *Like I want the best for you.*

"So?"

"I'm not best. Rachel's college educated. She can do better than a ranch hand. Besides, just like you, she'd go crazy living in the desert year-round."

"You could move to Rhode Island."

"There aren't many uses for cowboys or bull-fighters in Rhode Island."

"Maybe you could do construction work," Lauren persisted.

He figured he could pound nails for a living, but working cattle was his preference. He liked being a cowboy and whether or not P.T. would admit it, his boss needed him, especially if his health continued to fail. "Quit worrying about your old man and give Curly another try."

Clint decided he'd use the trip to Lake Powell

to prove to himself that Rachel was all wrong for him and he was all wrong for her. When they returned to the ranch, they'd both accept that the attraction between them was good-old-fashioned lust and nothing deeper.

Then what?

Hell if he knew.

"I COULD GET USED TO this life." Rachel lay on her stomach in the lounge chair on the sundeck of the *Red Devil*. The houseboat had been named after the rocky cliffs surrounding Lake Powell.

"Your back is burning." Clint reached for the sunscreen.

"Thanks." Rachel sighed when the first glop of cool lotion hit her heated skin. As soon as they'd arrived at the marina, she'd purchased a hot-pink bikini in the hotel gift shop while Clint sat through a basic course on houseboat management. Afterward, they'd motored across the lake, following a map the marina guide had provided, and dropped anchor in a secluded canyon. After eating sandwiches, they'd retreated to the upper deck to lie in the late-afternoon sun.

"That feels good," Rachel moaned as Clint's callused palms massaged the coconut-scented lotion into her skin. She peeked at his rugged face. He'd avoided direct eye contact with her all day. "You don't want to be here, do you?"

His hands pressed deeper into her muscle. "P.T. wanted you to see—"

"You came with me because it's what P.T. wanted."

Clint snapped the cap closed on the sunscreen then retreated to the deck rail where he stared at the shadows creeping across the canyon walls.

Rachel ogled his muscular physique. She loved the way his backside filled out a pair of Wranglers but he looked just as yummy in a pair of Hawaiian swim trunks. Dark hair covered his powerful pale legs and when he stretched his arms in the air, the muscles across his shoulders rippled and bulged.

Mesmerized by his half-naked body, Rachel sat up, forgetting she'd untied the strings on her bikini top. The material fell to her waist. Her gasp drew Clint's gaze to her exposed breasts.

Rachel's hands froze in the act of covering herself and less than a few seconds passed before she fumbled with the top. A stare down ensued, the air cracking with electricity. A tingling began in the pit of her stomach and spread through her limbs. The power Clint held over her body excited her.

Neither made a move until Clint flung his sunglasses onto the lounge chair and said, "I'm going for a swim." He walked to the rear of the boat and dove into the water.

Clutching her top, Rachel scrambled across the deck and peered over the edge. Clint's head popped above the water surface. "C'mon in! The water feels great!"

Rachel stepped back from view, retied the strings of her swimsuit, then descended the ladder on the side of the boat and eased her body into the cool water. Clint snuck up behind her and grasped her waist. "Feels good, doesn't it?" He whispered the words against her neck.

Rachel closed her eyes and sighed. She could get used to being in Clint's arms.

"How about a race?"

The question startled Rachel out of her reverie. "Race where?" They were in the middle of a massive lake.

Clint pointed into the distance. "See that rock?"

The small island was over a hundred yards out. She could handle it. "Last one there cooks supper." She splashed his face before swimming off. Clint followed, keeping pace with her. For a desert-dwelling cowboy he was a good swimmer. Ten yards from their goal, Clint surged ahead, then suddenly fell behind right before Rachel's fingertips touched the rock. He'd let her win.

Exhausted, she climbed from the water and stretched out on the warm stone. "I didn't know cowboys could swim."

Flashing a teasing grin, Clint asked, "How many cowboys do you know?"

"You're the first." Rachel shivered as Clint's gaze traveled over her body. That he wanted her was evident—the man gave off more signals than a third-base coach. So what held him back?

"If I ask you a question, will you give me an honest answer?" she said.

"Depends on the question."

"Why were you perturbed when you learned P.T. asked for my help with the rodeos?"

"I was worried you'd hurt P.T."

Shocked, Rachel protested, "Hurt him how?"

"I don't know. I blamed you for the rift between you and P.T."

"My father said he sent me away because he feared for my safety after my mother died." She still didn't understand why P.T. hadn't trusted himself with a small child.

"That doesn't make sense," Clint said.

"Did P.T. talk about my mother's death?"

"No, why?"

"I think maybe he blames himself for the horse accident she suffered." Once Rachel gathered her courage she'd ask her father for details about that day.

"P.T. was the first person in my life who cared about me," Clint said. "I was afraid that one morning he'd wake, change his mind and not want me." Clint's head rolled to the side and their mouths were inches apart. "Whatever happens between you and P.T., don't hurt him."

"Opening an old wound is bound to cause pain." She sighed. "I'll try to be understanding." If it hadn't been for that blasted kiss in the alley, Rachel wouldn't care about Clint's feelings and his relationship with her father.

"Another reason I didn't like the idea of you staying at the ranch was because you reminded me that despite my good intentions, I'd failed Lauren as a father."

"How have you failed Lauren?" Clint hadn't shared much about his relationship with his daughter and his comment piqued Rachel's curiosity.

"I've kept my daughter at a distance. I made a few token visits to California through the years and managed a twice-a-month phone call that lasted anywhere from thirty seconds to three minutes."

"Did Lauren and her mother cooperate with your attempts to visit?"

"Not really. Liz never forced Lauren to be with me."

"Tell me about Liz. Where did you two meet?"

"At a rodeo. Liz was there with a group of friends. We dated and a few months later Liz phoned with the news that she was pregnant."

"Has Lauren always lived with her mother in California?"

"Yep."

"Ah…you two aren't used to spending so much time together."

"'Fraid so." He chuckled. "Don't get me wrong, I was looking forward to getting to know my daughter better this summer, but I was nervous."

"About what?"

"That Lauren would see through me and realize I wasn't good enough to be her father."

"Why would you believe you aren't good enough?" Rachel struggled to reconcile the strong, stubborn bullfighter with the man lying next to her on the warm rocks.

Ignoring Rachel's question, Clint said, "Funny how life turns out. Who knows where I would have lived and what I'd be doing if I'd been adopted instead of placed in foster care."

"When were you given up for adoption?"

"At birth."

"Usually babies are easy to adopt out."

"They are, but I was born with an atrial septal defect."

"What's that?"

"A small hole between the upper chambers of my heart. The doctors closed the hole but no one wanted to risk raising a child who might suffer long-term health problems related to a heart defect."

"That's sad. Have you considered searching for your birth parents?"

"No. P.T. and Lauren are all the family I need."

Rachel stared at the clear blue sky, her heart aching. Clint's comment reminded her that she was the outsider. What would she have to do to earn the right to be included in P.T.'s small family circle?

"MMM, THAT SMELLS HEAVENLY." Rachel stepped into the galley kitchen, wearing a sundress that hugged her small bosom and flared at the hips before ending midthigh.

Forcing his eyes from her sexy outfit he said, "I hope you don't mind steak again, that's about all I know how to grill."

Rachel opened the fridge and removed a bag of lettuce and a fresh tomato. "I'll make a salad." She stood next to him, slicing the tomato, each movement of her arm sending a puff of shampoo-scented air drifting past his nose.

God, he wanted her. After searing both sides of the meat he turned the flame to the lowest setting. "I'm taking a quick—" cold "—shower." Ten minutes later he returned to the kitchen wearing a T-shirt and a pair of khaki shorts.

"A toast." Rachel held out a glass of red wine.

"To what?"

She clinked the rim of her glass against his. "To us and Five Star Rodeos."

"A lot can go wrong between now and the end of August."

"I'm confident the Boot Hill Rodeo next weekend will be another success."

He guzzled the wine, hoping the alcohol would shoot through his bloodstream and unravel the tight knot in his gut. "I forgot you don't eat much red meat. If you don't want a steak—"

"Steak is fine as long as it's well-done."

Clint moved his cut away from the flames while Rachel's steak finished cooking. He refilled his wineglass and forced his thoughts from Rachel—an impossible task when his mind wouldn't stop thinking about persuading her to join him in the bedroom after dinner.

He didn't want to hurt Rachel by misleading

her into believing their time on the boat together would change their relationship. The last thing he wanted to do was hurt P.T.'s daughter.

Maybe she only wants a brief fling.

You're a grown man. Rachel's a grown woman. What happens on the houseboat stays on the houseboat. He smiled.

"What's so amusing?" Rachel asked.

Unaware she'd been studying him, Clint muttered, "Nothing." He changed the subject. "I haven't gotten a text from Lauren all day. Have you?"

"Not a word. Want me to check in with her?"

"Sure. Ask her what she's doing tonight." He pretended interest in the steaks while Rachel texted with his daughter.

After a few minutes, Rachel set her phone aside. "Lauren's going to the movies with Shannon, then Shannon's staying overnight at the ranch and the other girls are returning in the morning to practice." Rachel's gaze connected with his and the heat in her blue eyes set his body on fire.

"Are you hungry?" he asked, his voice rough with emotion.

"Very." Her gaze fastened to his mouth.

"Your steak is almost done."

She set her wineglass on the counter then nuzzled his mouth. "The steaks can wait."

Inching the hem of her sundress higher on her thigh, Clint's fingertips caressed her skin. He drew in a sharp breath. "You're not wearing panties."

"No, I'm not."

Clint was no match for a pantiless woman. "Are you sure, Rachel?" At her silent nod, he turned off the grill, clasped her hand and led her down the hallway to the bedroom he'd picked when they'd boarded the houseboat.

"Wait." Rachel put the brakes on. "The sundeck."

"I'll meet you there." He hurried into the bedroom and grabbed protection from his toiletry kit then joined Rachel on the deck.

There were no other boats anchored in their private cove. The setting sun painted the sky in shades of pink and orange. Rachel stood by the two-person chaise lounge and lowered the spaghetti straps of her sundress. Clint helped her with the zipper and the dress pooled at her feet.

Wow. Rachel, naked, was an amazing sight. When he touched her breasts, her head fell back and she moaned, the sexy sound spurring Clint on. He replaced his hands with his mouth and she melted in his arms. She helped him shed his clothes, then they collapsed upon the chaise and he took her on a journey he prayed neither of them would regret.

FLOWERS. SOFTNESS. WARMTH.

Clint's senses slowly awakened, his fingers tightening against the firm thigh wedged between his legs, his body absorbing the heat of skin-to-skin contact.

Rachel.

He opened his eyes to a night sky sparkling with stars. A sigh escaped his chest and automatically he tightened his hold, as if keeping Rachel close warded off the guilt.

Making love had been a mistake. *A big mistake.* As much as he yearned to wake her with his kisses and caresses, he didn't dare. He hated the feeling of helplessness that had a choke hold on his emotions. He'd betrayed P.T.'s trust— having sex with Rachel was not how he had wanted Clint to look out for his daughter.

Clint soaked in the scent and feel of Rachel. In her arms he forgot she threatened everything dear to him—his place in P.T.'s heart and his home at Five Star Ranch. As a father with a daughter of his own he didn't want to be the man who stood in Rachel's way of reconciling with P.T.

Rachel deserves a chance to build a relationship with P.T.

Clint had had P.T. all to himself for years and Rachel was entitled to her father's love and attention, especially now with P.T.'s health in question. Clint worried that he didn't have the courage to step aside and allow Rachel and her father the space they needed to grow closer and heal their wounds.

"Hungry?"

The whispered question ended Clint's snarled thoughts. "I doubt the steaks are edible anymore."

Rachel propped herself on her elbows and smiled. The sparkle in her blue eyes set off another a surge of desire in his body. "I wasn't referring to food." Her mouth closed over Clint's and damned if all his good intentions didn't jump ship.

Chapter Eleven

"Rachel!" Lauren's frantic voice rang out as she zigzagged through the milling cowboys and cowgirls preparing for the Saturday afternoon events at the Boot Hill Rodeo.

"Whoa. Where's the fire?" Rachel's joke failed to erase the deer-in-the-headlights expression from Lauren's face. "What's wrong?" Rachel's first thought was Clint. She hadn't seen him in several hours but since returning from the houseboat on Lake Powell he was never far from her mind.

"Skylar isn't riding," Lauren said.

"Why?"

"Her dad had a heart attack this morning."

"Will he be okay?"

"Shannon said yes but the doctors are doing a medical procedure on him and Skylar's staying at the hospital with her mom."

Poor Skylar.

"What are we going to do, Rachel? We're one bull rider short."

A giant knot formed in Rachel's stomach. After Julie had dislocated her shoulder at the Canyon City Rodeo, Shannon had found a replacement—Hannah Buck from Tucson—but without Skylar they were still one competitor short.

"Let me take Skylar's place."

Rachel stared at Lauren in shock.

"You've seen me practice at the ranch. I'm ready."

Clint would never forgive Rachel if she allowed his daughter to compete without his permission. "Have you asked your father?"

"I'm not stupid, Rachel. I know my dad won't let me ride in a real competition."

At least the teen was honest. "I'm sorry, Lauren. I can't allow you to go behind your father's back."

"But they'll cancel the event."

"Let's talk with Shannon and the others." Rachel and Lauren joined the cowgirls who'd gathered near the bull pen.

"I'm guessing it's impossible to find another woman willing to ride in less than an hour." Rachel directed the comment to Shannon.

"Unlike barrel racers, female bull riders aren't a dime a dozen," Shannon said.

Wendy pointed to the bleachers where fans waved posters in support of the women's event. "We can't let them down."

"Maybe one of the barrel racers will help us out," Dixie chimed in.

Earlier in the day Rachel had overheard Shannon and Dixie chatting and discovered Shannon was paying Dixie a thousand dollars for each of the Five Star Rodeos Dixie competed in. Dixie had informed Shannon that she'd use the money to market her soaps online. If the women's event was canceled, Dixie wouldn't make her thousand dollars.

Rachel eyed the bulls in the holding pen. From a distance the animals appeared docile, but she'd witnessed firsthand their brutality.

You're in excellent physical condition.

You're strong.

Stubborn.

Tough.

More bullheaded than a bull.

An image of her father sitting on his hospital bed flashed before Rachel's eyes. Why was it so important that she not fail him? Did she really believe after all this time his feelings for her would change if the rodeos were a success this summer?

Are you willing to risk your life for a few words of appreciation from P.T.?

Dear God, help me. "Okay, here's what we're going to do." She motioned the women closer and they formed a tight circle. "I'm taking Skylar's place."

Silence greeted her statement. Then Dixie spoke. "You've never ridden a bull."

"Do not say a word to your father," Rachel told Lauren. "I'll switch my name with Skylar's right before the event." Pulse pounding in her veins, she spoke to Shannon. "I need a lesson in bull riding 101."

"You're not going for eight are you?" Shannon asked.

"I'm a fool but not that big of one," Rachel said.

"Okay, then. Wendy and I will secure the rope and make sure you've got a good grip. As soon as the bull clears the chute, release the bull rope and dive off."

"What's the best way to land?" Rachel expected a few bruises but wanted to avoid breaking her neck or snapping her spine, if possible.

"Depends on how you're thrown," Shannon said. "If you're headed face-first toward the dirt, twist at the waist so your shoulder takes the brunt of the impact. You'll get the wind knocked out of you, but you've got to roll away from the bull and get to your feet as quick as possible."

Block out the pain until I'm safe.

"The bullfighters will distract the bull so he doesn't charge," Kim said.

"What happens if the bull comes after me?"

"Run for the rails in a zigzag pattern and don't look back," Dixie said.

I can do this.

Shannon removed her riding gloves and handed them to Rachel. "Try these on. If they're too loose we'll find another pair."

"They fit fine."

"We're about the same size." Wendy handed Rachel her vest and protective headgear. "You want my chaps, too?"

"No." Rachel stood quietly while the other women tugged, pulled, snapped, tied and zipped her into the bull-riding gear.

"You're riding Sweet Water," Shannon said. "I'm not familiar with the bull so I can't help you with how he leaves the chute."

"Lean back, not forward." Kim secured the leather vest. "You don't want to fly over the bull's head."

"Should I try to keep my left hand in the air?" Rachel asked.

"I'd hang on with both hands if I were you and don't be concerned about disqualifying." Shannon stared into Rachel's eyes. "You're trying to survive, not win."

"Heavens, this thing is heavy." Rachel tugged on the vest. Hopefully the extra fifteen pounds of added weight would help her stay balanced. "I better sign in."

When she arrived at the sign-in table she said, "There's been a change in the women's bull-riding event."

"I know. Clint McGraw already informed us."

Clint had spoken to the rodeo officials? "Informed you of what?"

"That the women's event tonight has been canceled because one of the cowgirls didn't show."

Stunned, Rachel stood mute for a moment. Why would Clint cancel the event without consulting her first? *Because he wants to see you fail.*

No. A lump formed in Rachel's throat, threatening to choke her. *Not after their trip to Lake Powell. Not after spending time together...becoming closer...making love.*

"There's been a mistake," Rachel said.

"What kind of mistake?" the rodeo worker asked.

"We have a replacement for Skylar Riggins."

"Clint didn't mention a substitute."

"He didn't know."

"All right. Who's taking Skylar's place?"

"Me. Rachel Lewis."

"Where are you from, Rachel?"

"Providence, Rhode Island."

The woman's eyes twinkled. "Didn't think they had women's bull riding out East."

Rachel didn't comment.

"Okay, I'll inform the announcers and judges that the women's bull-riding event is still a go. Good luck."

"Thank you." Rachel returned to the chutes, but kept Clint's devious actions to herself, not wanting to upset the women before they rode.

"Are you scared, Rachel?" Lauren asked.

"Yep."

"Then don't ride. I don't want you to get hurt."

Lauren's confession tugged at Rachel's heartstrings. "I'll be fine. As soon as I see the right opening, I'm diving for safety."

The JumboTron flashed images of the women riding their bulls at the Canyon City Rodeo and after a minute the music died down and the announcer spoke.

"Folks, earlier tonight one of the female bull riders had to withdraw due to a family emergency."

Rachel scanned the cowboy-ready area searching for Clint. She spotted him speaking with his bullfighting partner Randy. Dressed in their colorful uniforms, their heads were bent in conversation.

"We'd planned to cancel the women's bull-riding event, but it looks as if a replacement for Skylar Riggins has been found, so we're gonna get to see these brave women compete after all!"

Clint's head snapped up and he glanced toward the chutes. His gaze landed on Rachel, his eyes widening when he noticed she wore rodeo gear. While the fans applauded and stomped their boots on the metal bleachers, Rachel engaged in a stare down with Clint. Shannon forced Rachel to break eye contact first.

"Be careful." Shannon's comment drew Rachel's attention to Sweet Water.

The black bull with flecks of white and brown around the neck appeared docile. *Be a nice boy.* Rachel climbed the rails and watched Shannon and Wendy work the rope around the animal. After they finished, Rachel gingerly settled onto Sweet Water's back, her blood pumping hard and fast through her veins.

"Give me your hand," Shannon said. She wrapped the rope around Rachel's fingers, pinning her hand in place—tight but not too tight.

"Will I be able to free my hand?" Rachel asked.

"The bull's bucking will loosen the rope. Remember, lean back and when you clear the rails, release your grip and push off."

"When do I nod to the gateman?" Rachel asked.

"Whenever you're ready." Shannon patted Rachel's thigh. "Go get 'em, cowgirl!"

CLINT STOOD TO THE RIGHT of the bull chute and fumed. Heart pounding like a jackhammer inside his chest, he couldn't take his eyes off Rachel sitting atop Sweet Water. The woman had lost her mind—the desert heat had finally driven her plum crazy.

"Folks, we've got six of the bravest women you'll ever run across in your lifetime. These cowgirls risk their lives for eight seconds of glory and a share of the pot. Riding first is Rachel Lewis from Providence, Rhode Island!"

A fear-induced sweat broke out across Clint's brow.

"Rachel's riding Sweet Water—a bull more sour than sweet," the announcer said.

Clint sent a hand signal to Randy, communicating that the rider was green. Randy signaled back that he'd move in close and distract the bull.

Damn it, Rachel. Her inexperience put Clint and Randy at greater risk once Rachel was thrown. Clint ran out of time to worry when the chute door opened and Sweet Water lurched into the arena.

The bull flung Rachel's body around like a rag doll—how the woman managed to keep her seat more than a second amazed Clint. While Randy waved his arms in front of Sweet Water's face, Clint watched Rachel twist her hand and loosen her hold on the rope. A moment later she flew through the air. As if viewing a slow-motion picture, her body floated past Clint, arms extended, legs tangled. She twisted at the last second, her shoulder slamming against the ground, absorbing the brunt of her fall. Rachel rolled twice before gaining control of her body.

Clint rushed into action, stepping between her and the bull. *Get up! Get up!*

In the extra seconds it took Rachel to stagger to her feet, Sweet Water turned on her. Randy shouted a warning but Clint had already inched closer to the bull, swatting its butt. Sweet Water changed direction and charged at Clint. He didn't have a chance to think—only react. He dove sideways, his thigh catching the tip of the bull's horn.

Jumping into the fray, Randy caught the bull's attention, enabling Clint to get to his feet. He checked over his shoulder, relieved to see Rachel had made it to safety.

After coaxing Sweet Water into the bull pen,

Randy trotted over to Clint. "You okay?" He pointed to the wet stain on Clint's shorts.

"Just a scratch. I'll have it checked after the last ride."

"Close call," Randy said. "We earned our money on that one."

No kidding. Rachel was lucky to be alive.

While the announcer droned on about the history of women's bull riding, Clint retreated behind the chutes and wrapped his leg with gauze. He willed his blood pressure to return to normal—fat chance when Rachel's ride played over and over in his mind. What if she'd been seriously injured? How would he have explained to P.T. that he'd failed to keep Rachel safe? Had she considered how her actions today might affect her father? P.T. had enough on his plate, fighting cancer. If Rachel had been hurt, P.T. would never forgive himself for asking her to come to Stagecoach for the summer.

And you would never forgive yourself, either.

"WHERE IS SHE?"

Rachel flinched when she heard the angry sound of Clint's voice outside the first-aid tent. Dan, the paramedic, had left her alone to check on a boy suffering from heat exhaustion. Seated on a cot with her left hand immersed in a bucket of ice water, she braced herself as the tent flap opened and Clint entered. Avoiding eye contact, she fastened her gaze to his chest. She'd put on a brave front for Lauren and the other women, but the bull ride had shaken Rachel to the core and she was an emotional mess.

"What happened?" He gestured to the bucket of ice water.

"I broke two fingers when I landed on the ground." She waited for Clint to speak but his mouth remained clamped shut. She dropped her gaze and her eyes widened at the sight of the red-stained bandage showing beneath his athletic shorts. "You got hurt."

"A nick." His tortured eyes bore into her for endless seconds, then he lowered his head and rubbed his brow. "Damn it, Rachel."

Was he scared because he cared about her and she could have been seriously injured or was he worried what P.T. would say if he got wind of her stunt?

"What the hell were you thinking, riding a bull?"

His anger fueled hers. "What were you thinking, canceling the women's event without my consent?"

The muscle in Clint's jaw pulsed with anger.

"I made a promise to my father and I will do everything in my power to keep that promise," she said.

"Even if it kills you?"

She sidestepped the question. "If I didn't know better I'd believe you were trying to sabotage my efforts to make the rodeos a success this summer."

"That's crazy." Clint avoided eye contact.

"I misjudged you," she said. "I assumed if my father trusted you to help him I could, too."

Face red, Clint didn't defend himself.

A sharp pain shot through her hand and Rachel decided now wasn't the time to go head-to-head with Clint. She motioned to his leg. "What happened?"

"Caught the tip of Sweet Water's horn when I jumped in front of you."

Oh, God. Her crazy actions today had not only put her life at risk but Clint's and his partner's, also. "I'm sorry. I never meant for—"

He moved closer, reached into the bucket and lifted her hand from the water. He gently touched her swollen fingers. "Did they give you something for pain?"

"Ibuprofen."

"Any news on Skylar's dad?" Clint returned her hand to the ice water.

"Not yet."

"Skylar will be back for the final rodeo." It was a statement, not a question.

"How did the rest of the women do?"

"Shannon's the only one who made it to eight. No one got hurt, except you."

And Clint.

"The girls are talking to the press right now and Lauren's checking with a local TV station about doing an interview with Shannon."

Rachel smiled. "Her pink hair intrigues the reporters."

"Yeah, well, I think her pink hair is ugly, but what do I know? I'm her dad."

"Have you talked with Mayor Ross?" As soon as she asked the question the tent flap opened and the mayor strolled in.

"By golly, Clint, we topped the Canyon City Rodeo attendance record." The mayor beamed. "Just as you promised, the women's bull-riding event played a big role in ticket sales."

Rachel wanted to protest that *she* deserved credit for today's success but kept her mouth shut.

Mayor Ross nudged Clint. "P.T. ought to have you running the show all the time."

What would the mayor think if he learned Clint had tried to cancel the women's event? Rachel silently fumed.

"How bad did you get hurt, missy?" Mayor Ross asked.

"Sprained a couple of fingers," Rachel lied.

"Glad it wasn't worse." The mayor tipped his

hat and left, bumping into the paramedic on the way out of the tent.

"Dan, would you check Clint's thigh?" Ignoring Clint's evil-eyed glare, Rachel lifted the ice bucket with her good hand and trailed after the mayor.

"Did you need stitches?" she asked ten minutes later when Clint stepped from the tent.

"No."

They stood in silence, Rachel's brain screaming for answers. Why were she and Clint always at odds? As she struggled to make sense out of his actions today, he walked off, leaving her feeling hollow and very much alone.

"RACHEL WAS REALLY brave today," Lauren said.

Brave? More like insane. He glanced at the kitchen clock in the cabin. Eleven-thirty. The day couldn't end fast enough for him. "Rachel was foolish to ride that bull. She could have been killed."

"I wanted to take Skylar's place but Rachel wouldn't let me."

"You what?" Clint couldn't believe his daughter would volunteer for such a foolhardy undertaking. *Lauren hopped on the back of a Harley with a stranger, didn't she?* Dealing with irrational females would turn Clint's hair gray by summer's end.

"I wouldn't have lasted eight seconds but I would have come close," Lauren boasted.

Clint's chest tightened as he visualized his daughter coming out of the chute on Sweet Water. "At least Rachel had sense enough to say no to you."

"I guess this summer isn't turning out so bad." Lauren yawned.

He chuckled and she playfully punched him in the stomach. "I still hate being stuck in the middle of nowhere all day, but I got to meet Shannon and her friends and I like helping Rachel with the rodeo stuff."

"You're turning into a cowgirl."

"Forget it, Dad. I'm not dying my hair back to brown. 'Night."

To check on Rachel or not?

The sick feeling Clint had gotten after his confrontation with Rachel in the first-aid tent earlier in the day still gnawed his gut.

I misjudged you. I assumed if my father trusted you to help him I could, too.

He'd disappointed a lot of people in his life but until Rachel's attack on his character, the only person he'd cared about impressing or pleasing had been P.T. Then Rachel had dropped out of the sky like a meteor crashing into his safe, secure world and challenging all he'd believed important to him.

Witnessing Rachel risk her life made Clint face the truth—he cared for her deeply. He hesitated using the word *love*—mostly because he'd experienced so little of it in his life that he wouldn't know love if it bit him in the backside. He didn't want to admit that Rachel had worked her way beneath his skin. If only the trip to Lake Powell had never happened. When he'd held Rachel in his arms he'd forgotten she was P.T.'s daughter.

His feelings for Rachel brought to the surface Clint's childhood insecurities. All these years Clint believed P.T.'s acceptance had given him the strength to hold those fears at bay. Had he been wrong? What if the key to his freedom wasn't P.T. but himself?

Clint left the cabin and made his way to the main house. He found the front door unlocked and entered the foyer. He opened his mouth to announce his presence, but the words became trapped in his throat when Rachel stepped from the bathroom at the end of the hall, wearing nothing but her birthday suit. Before his mind processed the details of her naked body, she disappeared into the bedroom.

Too stunned to do much more than stand in place and sweat, he closed his eyes and images of making love to Rachel on the houseboat flashed through his mind. A gasp interrupted his daydream and Clint's eyes flew open. Rachel had emerged from the bedroom wearing a cotton robe.

"I knocked but—"

"I was in the shower."

"Thought you might need help." He motioned to her injured hand.

"I took the splint off because the tape was dirty."

They met in the middle of the hallway and Clint clasped her injured hand, rubbing his thumb across the swollen knuckles. With damp hair and no makeup she looked vulnerable and barely older than Lauren. "Where's the splint?"

"In here."

He followed her into the bedroom. Clothes were strewn across the floor. Cosmetics, lotions and fingernail polish cluttered the top of the dresser.

"What are you smiling at?" she asked.

"I never pegged you as a messy person."

"I'm not—" she sat on the edge of the bed "—but things have been so crazy I haven't had time to clean."

Clint joined her, the mattress dipping beneath his weight. Their shoulders bumped. The scent of citrus shampoo filled the air. Gently, he arranged her broken fingers in the splint then tore off strips of medical tape and immobilized her fingers. "Lauren said she volunteered to ride but you wouldn't let her."

"I'd never allow her to take such a risk."

The heat from Rachel's body warmed his side and Clint fought the urge to lay her down and explore with his hands what his eyes had viewed moments ago.

Her stomach grumbled, the noise propelling him off the bed. "Get dressed in your pajamas while I fix you a snack."

Five minutes later Rachel entered the kitchen.

"I warmed a can of soup and made turkey sandwiches." He placed the food on the bistro table overlooking the patio.

"You're staring," she said.

"Sorry." He had a heck of time blocking Rachel's naked body from his mind. Clint pointed to the food. "Eat, and then I'll tuck you into bed."

"Do I get a bedtime story?" Rachel's eyes simmered with heat.

If things were different, Clint would do a hell of a lot more than read to Rachel.

Chapter Twelve

Rachel paused outside the bedroom door and flashed a shaky smile at Clint. Now that she'd showered and eaten, the full extent of her reckless actions today had finally sunk in, leaving her feeling vulnerable and scared. Never before had she questioned her judgment, but her decision to ride Sweet Water at the Boot Hill Rodeo cast serious doubts on her intelligence.

Not only had she put her and the bullfighters' lives at risk, if she'd been trampled to death her father, Clint, Lauren and the lady bull riders would have had to live with guilt the rest of their lives—each blaming themselves for not stopping her.

Clint leaned a shoulder against the door frame. His brown-eyed stare made her skin tingle, the sensation spreading through her limbs, masking the dull throb in her broken fingers. Her breathing grew shallow as she imagined Clint's hands caressing her skin… His fingers tunneling through her hair... His mouth teasing her lips...her breasts.

Why Clint? Why did she yearn for his love—a man who'd replaced her in her father's heart? A man who wanted to see her fail.

She shook her head, her thoughts too jumbled to sort through. Right now...right here... Clint wasn't the enemy. She wanted to lie in his arms and forget everything but the feel of his body making love to hers. She pressed her palm to his chest, the thump of his heart comforting. Lightly she brushed her lips over his mouth. Once. Twice. When he didn't pull away she stood on tiptoe and leaned closer.

Did Clint sense how much she needed him?

His arms pulled her close then he cupped her fanny, snuggling her pelvis against the hardness beneath the zipper of his jeans. *He wants me.* A tiny thrill skated through her, but the emotion was short-lived when he released her.

"What's wrong?"

"We can't do this." Instead of driving her away, Clint's words drew Rachel closer. He dragged a hand through his hair and reined in his arousal.

"Make love to me." Her whispered plea chipped away at the stone wall around his heart.

"I promised P.T. I'd protect you."

"Protect me from what?"

Not *what... Who.* Was Clint trying to protect Rachel or himself from getting hurt? "I meant—"

"I've spent twenty-two years of my life without a father to guide me. P.T. hasn't earned the right to tell anyone, especially you, to watch over me."

"Especially me?"

"We both know you're more P.T.'s child than I am."

"You're his biological daughter. I'm the teenager he rescued from the streets."

"My father gave you a home and banished me from mine."

"I don't want to argue about this, Rachel." Clint didn't care to acknowledge that P.T. had treated Rachel unfairly. He didn't want to accept that the man he admired most in life had done his daughter wrong. "Are you driving to Phoenix tomorrow to visit P.T.?"

After a tense moment, she said, "Yes. Do you want to come along?"

"Sure." Visiting P.T. in person would strengthen his resolve to keep Rachel at a distance. "What will you say when he asks about your fingers?"

"I'll make up something." She waved a hand in the air. "My father doesn't know me well enough to guess when I'm lying or telling the truth."

The bedroom door closed in Clint's face.

CLINT SWUNG HIS TRUCK into a stall at the medical center, shifted into Park but left the motor running. The trip from Stagecoach to Phoenix had been the longest of Rachel's life. Neither of them had much to say after she'd closed the bedroom door in Clint's face the previous night. She hated the tension between them and wanted to apologize but wasn't sure what for— begging him to make love to her or being P.T.'s daughter?

"Let's set the ground rules before we go in," Clint said.

"Ground rules?"

"You don't mention that I'm giving Lauren bull-riding lessons and I won't correct whatever story you tell P.T. about your broken fingers."

"Fair enough." Rachel climbed out of the truck. When Clint rounded the hood, she said, "I don't understand how P.T. hasn't heard about the women's rough-stock event being added to the rodeos."

Clint held the clinic door open for Rachel. A blast of refrigerated air engulfed her and she shivered.

"Maybe P.T. does know about the bull riding," Clint said, pushing the button on the elevator.

"Wouldn't he have called one of us to protest?"

"Maybe not. We're breaking attendance records and that's money in the bank."

"In other words, once the rodeo in Piney Gorge is over all hell is going to break loose?"

"That's my guess." They rode the elevator to the third floor. As soon as they stepped off, Rachel spotted P.T. in the hall lounge.

"You've got company, Mr. Lewis." A nurse pointed to Clint and Rachel.

P.T.'s gaze landed on Clint first and he smiled. Rachel ignored the twinge of envy pinching her side. Her father looked her way but the smile slid off his face as soon as he noticed the splint on her fingers.

"What happened?" P.T. shuffled down the corridor.

"Let's talk in your room." Rachel entered first and went straight to the recliner.

Clint shut the door and leaned against the wall while P.T. sat on the edge of the bed facing Rachel. "Well?"

"I broke two fingers," she said.

"What happened?"

Here goes nothing. "I went for a horseback ride and fell—" Rachel rushed to P.T.'s side as the blood drained from his face. "Dad, are you okay?"

"P.T.?" Clint joined her at the bed.

"You have no business riding a horse," her father admonished.

P.T.'s anger shocked Rachel.

"And you." P.T. pointed at Clint. "I told you to watch out for my daughter."

"Don't yell at Clint. This wasn't his fault."

"The hell you say," P.T. growled.

"I didn't tell Clint I went riding." Another lie. The last thing she wanted was to get Clint in trouble with her father. "May I speak to P.T. in private?" Without a word Clint vanished from the room.

"Dad, why are you upset over a couple of broken fingers?"

P.T. stared into space. "I don't want to lose you the way I lost your mother."

His confession stole the air from Rachel's lungs. This was the closest her father had come to telling her he loved her. She waited for him to continue but he remained silent, staring unseeingly across the room. Aunt Edith had been the only person to offer Rachel an explanation about the day her mother had died. Now Rachel wanted to hear the details from her father. "What are you talking about?"

"Anne...your mother, she never wanted to

live on the ranch. She was a city girl. I promised her after you were born that I'd find a way to buy a small house in Yuma for the two of you to live."

Aunt Edith had never said a word about Rachel's mother hating the ranch. "Did Mom ever get her house?"

"I saved enough for a down payment but the business suffered a setback and I used the money to cover debts. Your mother found out I spent our savings and we argued." P.T. rubbed a hand down his face. "I wasn't very sympathetic to her complaints. She felt isolated on the ranch and worried about you not having friends to play with." A tear escaped her father's eye.

Caught off guard by her father's vulnerability, Rachel's throat tightened.

"I accused Anne of being weak." P.T.'s gaze dropped the floor. "Of not having what it takes to be a rancher's wife."

"Did you mean what you said?" Rachel asked.

"No! I loved your mother with all my heart." He shook his head. "Later that day after we'd argued, Anne put you down for a nap then saddled the most spirited horse in the barn and took him for a run in the desert. I didn't know she'd left until you came out of the house calling for her."

Rachel could imagine her father's panic.

"When I discovered Tracer's empty stall, I sent you to your room to play then went after your mother." Her father shuddered, his voice heavy with pain. "I found her lifeless body a short distance from the house. She'd broken her neck when she'd been thrown from the horse."

Dear God, had she known the whole truth about her mother's death Rachel would never have used the same scenario to explain her broken fingers. Learning her parents had argued prior to her mother's accident made the event even more tragic.

"I'm the reason you lost your mother, Rachel."

Her father's confession left her with more questions than answers.

"But you still sent me away. Why?"

"Isn't it obvious?"

Not to Rachel.

"I couldn't bring your mother back to life for you, but I could give you the life your mother wanted you to have—a life in the city with lots of friends."

Although sympathy for her father gathered steam inside Rachel, she refused to let him off the hook. She needed time to process what he'd told her, but there was one more question she wanted an answer to. "I understand your reason for sending me to live with Aunt Edith, but that doesn't explain why you stopped being my father."

Her sharp words snapped P.T.'s head back. "I never stopped being your father."

"Oh, really?"

P.T. shook his fist in the air. "I knew everything you did, young lady!" He sucked in a deep breath, his face red. "You gave Edith fits about your curfew." He poked himself in the chest. "I'm the one who set your curfew. Ten o'clock weekdays and midnight weekends."

Dumbstruck, Rachel stared.

"And I insisted Edith allow you to quit piano lessons so you could try out for the volleyball team."

Rachel's mind raced back to junior high school. She'd desperately wanted to become involved in a sport but her aunt had believed playing a musical instrument would serve Rachel better. Then one morning out of the blue Aunt Edith had placed a pair of knee pads on the kitchen table along with a signed parental consent form to try out for the volleyball team. Rachel had been over-the-moon happy, offering to do her chores for a whole month without receiving an allowance. All along she'd had her father to thank for her aunt's sudden change of heart.

Why didn't you reach out to me, Dad? "I made the varsity team in high school."

P.T. grinned. "I know. You got the award for most valuable player your senior year."

Instead of making her feel better, the fact her father had kept tabs on her activities from long distance made her feel sad and alone.

"You could have come to one of my volleyball games."

"There were always things needing to be done at the ranch. Animals had to be fed and the rodeos…" His voice trailed off.

"The truth, Dad. Why did you keep your distance from me?" Right before her eyes, P.T. aged ten years—the wrinkles bracketing his mouth deepened and the loose folds of skin around his eyes drooped.

"I stayed away because I believed you didn't want anything to do with me, and I knew if I'd asked you to visit the ranch you'd refuse."

"I probably would have," she said. "But the choice should have been mine."

For years she'd resented her father for abandoning her when in truth he'd sent her away because he'd wanted to fulfill the promise he'd broken to Rachel's mother. Now what? Where did their relationship go from here? And what about the apology she craved from her father— did the words even matter?

She studied P.T. through fresh eyes and with a renewed sense of hope. The uplifting thought took a sober turn when she realized that her father's revelations wouldn't matter if he didn't beat his cancer. "What have the doctors said about your progress?"

A knock sounded on the door, and Clint walked into the room. Rachel's question went unanswered when P.T. changed the subject.

"Lauren didn't come with you today?"

Clint's turn to lie.

"She watched movies until two in the morning and was sound asleep when Rachel and I left."

"What did you think of Lake Powell, Rachel?"

Her gaze clashed with Clint's and they both looked away quickly.

"The area's breathtaking." Rachel moseyed over to the window and stared at the courtyard below, hoping P.T. would drop the subject of their minivacation on the houseboat.

"I hear you broke attendance records at Boot Hill."

"Who told you?" Rachel gasped.

"Jack Ross phoned last night and said he was pleased with the PR Five Star used to promote the Boot Hill Rodeo." P.T. nodded to Rachel. "What sort of gimmicks are you using?"

"The usual," Rachel said. "Flyers, newspaper articles, a few radio spots."

"We never used radio before." P.T. looked at Clint.

"That was Rachel's idea," Clint said. "The listeners love hearing from the rodeo contestants."

"What cowboys have been interviewed? C. J. Rodriguez?"

"We don't want to tire you out from too much talk." Rachel stood. "Before we head back to Stagecoach can we get you any—"

"I don't need a thing. They treat me like a king here."

Instead of heading for the door, Rachel detoured, stopping to give her father a hug. The gesture surprised P.T. but a few seconds later she felt his arms surround her. Tears burned her eyes and she scurried from the room, allowing Clint a private goodbye.

"Everything okay between you and my daughter?" P.T. asked.

Startled by the question, Clint dropped his gaze to the tips of his boots. "We're fine, P.T."

"You haven't been the same since Rachel showed up at the ranch."

"What do you mean?"

"We used to talk about everything, but you barely have two words to say to me now."

Clint opened his mouth to deny the charge then changed his mind.

"If not for you I would never have had the courage to ask my daughter to help me this summer."

"Why did you ask Rachel to run Five Star Rodeos and not me?"

"I didn't know how else to show my daughter that I loved her." P.T. held Clint's gaze. "There's no way I would have put Rachel in charge if you hadn't been there to watch over her and fix her mistakes."

"You could have made things easier on everyone if you'd told Rachel that you loved her."

P.T. quirked an eyebrow.

Okay, so they both sucked at communicating their feelings to those they cared about.

"What happens between you and Rachel after this summer?" Clint asked.

P.T. shrugged. "I don't know, but the one thing that's keeping my hope alive is you."

"Me?"

"If Rachel decides to never see me again at least I know I have you."

Clint's throat swelled with emotion. He and P.T. kept their feelings close to the vest. Clint preferred to show how much he cared through his loyalty and hard work, but P.T.'s confession reassured Clint that he'd always have a place at Five Star Ranch if he wanted.

"Make no mistake, Clint. You saved me more than I saved you. I might have taken you in all those years ago but you gave me a reason to go on when I'd believed Rachel was lost to me for good."

"Now you have your daughter back, so—"

"I need you even more."

Damn. Clint's eyes stung.

"As far as I'm concerned, you're both my children and I love you equally."

Unable to speak, Clint walked over to the window and willed his emotions to settle down. "I've always wished you were my real father."

"I reckon that's a good thing seeing how I've always wished you were my real son." P.T. cleared his throat. "You'd better get going. Rachel's probably champing at the bit in the lobby."

Clint cut across the room but stopped short of the door. "I'm sorry I never told you how much I appreciate you being there for me through the years."

"Same goes for me, son."

Feeling better about his relationship with P.T., Clint left the room, closing the door softly behind him. He stepped into the elevator and punched the button for the lobby. If only he felt better about his feelings for Rachel.

"HUNGRY?" CLINT ASKED when the elevator door opened in the lobby.

"Starving." Even though she'd done nothing physical today, Rachel's emotions had undergone a strenuous workout. She followed Clint across the parking lot.

"There's a diner at the edge of town. Everything on the menu is homemade."

"I'm game."

At five in the afternoon Hot Mama's Café was slammed. "You won't be disappointed," Clint said when they stepped inside the restaurant.

A large woman behind the lunch counter called Clint's name. "Can't get enough of Mama's cookin'?" Pointing to the stools in front of her, she said, "Sit your handsome face right here."

As soon as they were seated, the woman asked, "You got a new girlfriend, Clint?"

"Rachel, I'd like you to meet Maybelle Patterson. She owns Hot Mama's Café. Maybelle, this is P.T.'s daughter, Rachel Lewis."

"Nice to meet you," Rachel said.

"Likewise." The café owner spoke to Clint. "The usual?"

"What's his usual?" Rachel asked.

"Fried Spam patties with a side of homemade potato salad."

"Eew!" Rachel laughed.

"I ate a lot of Spam as a kid." Clint grinned. "Guess it grew on me."

"What's the special today, Maybelle?" Rachel asked.

"Chicken potpie. Pastry shell's made from scratch."

"I'll have the special and a diet cola."

Maybelle glanced at Clint. "Water's fine," he said. After Maybelle walked off, he said, "You've never eaten Spam."

"God, no. What's in that stuff anyway?"

"Pork shoulder and ham."

"You said you ate a lot of it as a kid." Rachel wanted to talk about someone else's childhood instead of thinking of her own.

"Most of the foster homes I lived in stockpiled Spam because it was cheap."

"You mentioned that you'd never searched for your birth parents, but don't you want to know why they gave you away?" Shoot, she'd wondered most of her life why P.T. hadn't wanted to keep her with him.

"My parents didn't want me—what more do I need to know?"

"There might have been special circumstances or—"

"My mother was seventeen. My father sixteen. I had health issues."

"They were awfully young to take care of a baby, especially one with medical needs. Maybe neither of them had family willing to help raise you."

"You don't have to defend my birth parents, Rachel. I don't harbor any animosity toward them. I'm sure they had valid reasons for giving me up, but it doesn't change the fact that I don't feel any deep need to have a relationship with them."

"What if they want to get to know you?"

"If you're so insistent I reach out to my birth parents, what's your excuse for keeping your distance from P.T. until now?"

Touché.

"Here you go." Maybelle set their meals on the counter then stared expectantly.

Rachel sampled her potpie. "This is tasty."

Maybelle beamed. "It's my daddy's recipe."

"Spam's as good as ever," Clint said.

"Stop by Mama's more often. I only see you once or twice a year."

"You open a Hot Mama's Café in Yuma and I'd be there every day." Clint grinned.

"I'm too old to run more'n one business." She smiled at Rachel. "He's been comin' on to me for years, honey, but I swore off cowboys when one broke my heart." Maybelle sashayed back to the kitchen.

"Do you think P.T. knows about the women's rough-stock events?" Rachel asked between bites.

"He would have raked me over the coals if Mayor Ross had mentioned it during their phone call." Clint swallowed a bite of food. "Did you and P.T. settle things this afternoon?"

"I learned why he sent me away after my mother died." She believed her father would never have found the courage to contact her if he hadn't come down with cancer.

"You going to tell me or is it a big secret?"

"My mother had worried about me growing up on the ranch isolated from other kids. P.T. wanted to fulfill my mother's wish that I be raised in a city where I'd have the opportunity to make lots of friends."

"That doesn't explain why he didn't raise you."

"He was afraid I'd reject him if he tried to become involved in my life."

"Sounds like P.T. asked you to return to Stagecoach because he's trying to make amends for the past. You should give him a chance."

"Who are you to tell me what to do when you won't give your birth parents a chance?"

They finished their meals in silence.

Chapter Thirteen

Thank God.

Rachel sighed in relief when Clint turned the truck onto the gravel road leading to the Five Star Ranch. After they'd left Hot Mama's Café, he'd become quiet and withdrawn. She worried that she'd pressed him too hard about his birth parents. What had gotten into her? Rachel stared at the brown desert whizzing by and wished with all her heart that she and Clint had met under different circumstances.

She yearned for a chance to discover if what she felt for Clint was strong enough to survive whatever lay ahead for her and her father. Making love to Clint had been an incredible experience—one she believed she'd never find with any other man. The explosive feelings Clint's kisses and caresses triggered in her went beyond explanation. They'd shared more than their bodies on the houseboat at Lake Powell, and her heart insisted that Clint had been as moved by their lovemaking as she'd been. When their gazes had connected, the warmth in his brown eyes had reached deep into her soul. There was no doubt in her mind that he cared about her.

If he cares why isn't he helping more with the rodeos?

Until now Rachel had ignored the tiny voice in her head that insisted Clint hoped she'd disappoint P.T. What would he gain if Rachel failed in her duties to her father?

"I apologize if I was out of line this afternoon. I didn't mean to stick my nose into your business," she said.

Clint's grip on the wheel tightened. "Don't worry about it."

How could she not worry when he'd given her the silent treatment the past thirty miles? "You haven't said more than ten words since we left Yuma."

"I've got a lot on my mind."

"Are you concerned about the Piney Gorge Rodeo?"

"No."

"Lauren?"

"No."

She hated playing the guessing game. "P.T.?"

"Leave it be, Rachel."

Not possible. "Then I must be the reason you're upset."

He slammed on the brakes and the truck skidded to a halt. He shifted into Park and stared out the windshield. "I owe you an apology."

"You do?"

"I overstepped my bounds at the Boot Hill Rodeo."

She understood why he'd canceled the bull riding—there hadn't been enough women to compete. But she didn't understand... "Why didn't you confer with me first before you spoke to the rodeo officials?"

Seconds passed and Clint remained silent.

"Talk to me, Clint. Tell me what's going on with you. I thought our time on the houseboat—"

"P.T. would be madder than a hornet if he knew I took advantage of you."

"Took advantage of me? I'm a grown woman capable of deciding who I have sex with."

"P.T. expected me to look out for you."

The conversation was getting sidetracked. "I don't need a protector. Besides, my father's concern comes a little too late in the game."

"P.T. did what he believed was best for you."

"Yes, he did, but that doesn't excuse him from not reaching out to me until his cancer diagnosis." Hurt that Clint took P.T.'s side, Rachel lashed out. "You're making excuses for P.T. because you're looking for a way to justify your bad parenting."

Clint's gaze clashed with hers, but Rachel was on a roll and refused to stop. "At first I was jealous that P.T. had taken you in and treated you as a son. Once I learned about your tough childhood in foster care, I conceded that you deserved to have someone care about you."

The muscle along Clint's jaw pulsed with anger. "And this relates to my relationship with Lauren how?"

"Your fear of losing P.T.'s love is keeping you from being the kind of father you should have been to Lauren through the years."

He stared at Rachel as if she'd grown two heads.

"You made a token effort to see Lauren because P.T. rode your back, not because you wanted to."

"Not true. Lauren's my daughter. I love her."

"Of course you love her. But you're scared she won't love you back. Like all the other foster parents you were forced to live with, you believe Lauren will find you lacking." Clint's face glowed red and his chest heaved with anger.

Rachel had come this far, she might as well put everything on the table. "P.T. accepted you, faults and all." And Rachel suspected Clint would do everything in his power to keep his relationship with P.T. from changing, which included turning his back on her and what they'd shared on the houseboat.

"What happens when P.T.'s gone, Clint? What if he doesn't survive his fight with cancer? Who will be there for you after you've kept everyone else at arm's length?"

A full minute passed before Clint shifted into Drive and eased his foot off the brake. The truck lurched forward, spewing gravel into the air. At least Rachel had found out now—before she'd made a fool of herself and confessed she'd fallen in love with Clint—that no matter how much he insisted he cared about her, there was only one person he would ever trust with his heart: P.T.

She had to accept that Clint, Lauren and P.T. were a family—Rachel was the outsider. In the end, she'd have to be satisfied with making peace with her father and leaving his family intact—a family she yearned to be a part of.

"Something's up," Clint said as he pulled into the ranch yard and Rachel watched his daughter race toward the truck. Clint opened the driver-side door. "What's the matter?"

"It's Dixie."

"What about Dixie?" Rachel unsnapped her seat belt.

Lauren's gaze swung between her father and Rachel. "She can't ride in the Piney Gorge Rodeo."

"Why not?" Rachel asked.

"Dixie's pregnant."

Pregnant? Rachel stared at her broken fingers. She was in no shape to take Dixie's place. Even if she was, Rachel wasn't sure she had the courage to ride another bull—not after she knew what to expect when the chute door opened. "I'll call Shannon, although I imagine she's already looking for a replacement." There had to be a rancher's daughter in the area willing to take Dixie's spot.

"I'll ride," Lauren said.

Clint's mouth sagged open, then snapped shut with a decisive click. "No, you won't."

"I'm eighteen. You can't tell me what to do." Lauren turned to Rachel. "Put me on the roster."

"The hell she will!" Clint roared.

Rachel had witnessed Clint's face turn white more than once this past week as his daughter honed her bull-riding skills. His reaction reminded Rachel of P.T.'s fear that harm would come to her if she'd remained at the ranch after her mother had died. Rachel didn't want history to repeat itself. If Lauren got injured, Clint would blame himself then keep Lauren at arm's length because he didn't trust himself to do what was in her best interests. Clint and Lauren's relationship had come a long way this summer and Rachel refused to allow the final rodeo to ruin their progress.

"Let's discuss this as rational adults," Rachel said.

"Even Rachel acknowledges that I'm an adult." Lauren flashed a smug grin.

"You don't have enough experience." Clint removed his Stetson and banged it against his thigh.

"I've been practicing for weeks. Look how much I've improved on Curly."

"Curly is old and docile. The rodeo bulls are meaner and quicker." Clint shook his head. "Doesn't matter how I feel, your mother won't—"

Lauren stomped several feet away. "You and Mom can't stop me from competing."

"This isn't your father's decision to make, Lauren." Rachel hated being the one to disappoint the teen, but in good conscience, she could not allow the eighteen-year-old to put herself in danger. "I'm in charge of the rodeos."

"What are you saying?" Lauren asked.

"I won't allow you to ride. I'm sorry."

"This totally sucks!" Lauren raced to the cabin, slamming the door behind her.

"Thanks," Clint said.

"No problem. I'm used to being the bad guy." Rachel was determined not to allow a setback this late in the game ruin the overall success of the rodeos. "I'll be in the house if you need me." Though Clint had already made it abundantly clear that he didn't.

"LAUREN'S IMPROVED A LOT," Shannon said. The female bull rider stood with Rachel watching Lauren climb onto a bull. Shannon and her friends had made a pit stop at the ranch to practice for the Piney Gorge Rodeo tomorrow.

No matter that Rachel and Clint had told Lauren she wouldn't be competing, the stubborn teen had trained all week then had worked out on the bucking machine in the barn. Lauren had left Clint no choice but to remain by her side while she practiced. Not even his permanent scowl had deterred his daughter.

The chute opened and Curly vaulted into the pen. Lauren hit the dirt after three seconds.

"Wrangler called me," Shannon said.

"Wrangler as in the jean company?"

"Yep, they said if I win tomorrow they'll sponsor a bull-riding tour for me next season."

"That's fantastic." The pressure on Rachel intensified. She had to find a way to keep the women's event from being canceled. "Did you hear from the girl in Nebraska?"

"She's not interested in taking Dixie's place."

Great. Rachel stared into the distance at the swath of pink cutting across the evening sky. Her back was against the wall. She didn't want to fail the town of Piney Gorge or Mayor Larsen, or ruin Shannon's chance at a Wrangler sponsorship. And Five Star Rodeos needed another record-setting attendance event to put enough money in the bank to support the sanctuary ranch for the upcoming year.

Lauren came out of the chute on a different bull. This time she clung to the animal for six seconds before landing on her fanny. She staggered to her feet, wincing as she brushed the dust from her backside. Enough was enough.

"Clint! Lauren!" Rachel shouted. "Can I have a word with you two?"

Father and daughter cut across the pen.

"We haven't found a replacement for Dixie, so I've decided to ride," Rachel said.

"No way." Lauren propped her hands on her hips. "I'm better than you. I should ride."

Clint ignored his daughter's outburst. "You can't ride with broken fingers."

"I hold the rope with my right hand. I'll be fine." Fearing she'd back down to pressure, Rachel walked off. Two seconds after she'd entered the house the front door blew open. Clint stood on the welcome mat, steam spewing from his ears.

"You're not riding tomorrow." He stepped inside the foyer and shut the door.

"I'm not your daughter." *And you made it clear that I'm not your significant other.* "You can't tell me what to do."

"Mayor Larsen will understand if—"

"I'm calling the shots, Clint. Not you."

"P.T. wouldn't want you to ride."

"My father asked me to return to Stagecoach to manage the summer rodeos. That's what I'm doing."

"You got off easy the first time, Rachel. I won't allow you to risk another injury."

"Be careful or I might believe you care about me."

In a move so quick Rachel gasped, Clint pinned her to the door, his body blocking her escape. "Making love to you earned me the right to be concerned about your safety." His mouth inched closer, scrambling Rachel's brain until she couldn't form a coherent thought.

"Damn it, Rachel. I do care about you."

Tell me you love me and I won't ride.

The words never came.

How could Clint have made love to her and not recognized she wasn't a threat to him? Whether she succeeded or not in proving she was the better candidate to run her father's business, she'd never take what he'd worked for years to earn. The future of Five Star Rodeos belonged to Clint, not Rachel.

Clint's mouth inched closer, but Rachel turned her head and his lips brushed her cheek. No more kisses—kisses made leaving too difficult.

"'Night, Clint."

The sound of the front door closing released a flood of tears from her eyes.

"LADIES AND GENTS, we've packed the stands today for Piney Gorge's first-ever women's rough-stock event. For those of you who've never seen a cowgirl ride a bull, you're in for a wild time!" Applause followed the announcer's spiel.

"Rex, the clown, is gonna show you folks what to expect." Catcalls and whistles erupted when a rodeo clown, wearing cowboy boots and a low-cut 1890s saloon dress with pantaloons and a big blond wig, strolled in front of the crowd. Following the clown, a cowboy led a small calf on a rope. When the clown attempted to climb onto the calf, the animal moved and the clown landed on his fanny, ruffled skirt covering his head.

"You sure about this?" Shannon asked Rachel. The women stood next to the bucking chutes.

"Positive." Maybe if she repeated the mantra in her head enough she'd believe it. "Have you seen Clint?"

"He and Randy are already inside the arena."

Clint had been avoiding Rachel all day. If not for Lauren's incessant chatter on the way to Piney Gorge, the hour-and-a-half drive would have been the longest of Rachel's life. Once they'd reached the fairgrounds, she and Clint had gone their separate ways.

"Where's Lauren?" Rachel asked.

"I don't know. Maybe she went to get a hot dog." Shannon exchanged long stares with a rodeo contender in the cowboy-ready area.

"Who's that?" Rachel asked.

"Gavin Tucker."

The name sounded familiar. "Wasn't he the cowboy Dixie hung out with at the other two rodeos?"

"Yep, that's him. He recently got out of the army."

"Is he the father of Dixie's baby?" Rachel asked.

"Don't know."

Rachel returned her attention to the other women gathering near the chutes. Wendy prepared to ride first. The announcer's voice droned on in the background but Rachel blocked out the sound when she noticed Clint and his partner decked out in their colorful outfits. Rachel drew comfort knowing Clint would do his best to protect her from the bull once she was thrown.

Wendy climbed the chute rails and straddled Tootsie, a black bull. Shannon and a rodeo helper looped the rope around the animal. Once Wendy was satisfied with her grip, she bobbed her head and the gateman opened the chute door. She lasted five seconds before sailing over Tootsie's head. When she hit the ground, she tucked her body and performed a somersault before coming to her feet. The flashy landing earned her a standing ovation.

Up next, Rachel donned her riding vest and helmet, then retreated to the shadows to gather her composure. Turning her back to the group, she took deep, calming breaths in an attempt to subdue the anxiety building in her.

"Folks, we got a glitch in the lineup tonight. Looks like Lauren McGraw is taking the place of Dixie Cash who's withdrawn from the event for personal reasons. Lauren's from Los Angeles, California. A city girl turned country!"

The blood drained from Rachel's face. She whipped off her headgear and scanned the bull chutes, searching for Lauren. Dressed in protective gear, she sat on a bull in the very last chute.

"Ms. McGraw's about to tangle with Dancer!"

"Stop! Wait!" Rachel raced toward the chute. Too late. The door opened and Lauren disappeared from view.

Heart pounding with fear, Rachel watched Lauren struggle to keep her seat on Dancer. She wanted to glance at Clint but she couldn't take her eyes off Lauren. Dancer twisted right and Lauren slid sideways but managed to regain her balance before the next buck.

God, please keep her safe.

Dancer's next buck threw Lauren forward, but the teen kept her balance and the crowd went wild.

C'mon, Lauren. You can do it.

Dancer fought hard but Lauren gave no quarter and the buzzer sounded. Lauren had made it to eight before a crowd of thousands, but Rachel refused to enjoy the girl's success, because Dancer was making it impossible for Lauren to dismount.

Randy waved his arms in front of the bull's face while Clint approached from the side and helped untangle the rope from Lauren's hand. Once freed, she vaulted into her father's arms. Clint whisked Lauren to safety while Randy coaxed Dancer back to the stock pens.

"Well, folks, it looks like Lauren McGraw made a name for herself tonight. We'll call her Hollywood after the show she put on. Lauren's the first female bull rider to make it to eight on Dancer. Let's see how the judges scored her." A few seconds passed and the crowd cheered when Lauren's score flashed on the JumboTron. "Hollywood earned herself an 82! Not bad for her first rodeo."

As soon as Lauren returned to the cowboy-ready area, Rachel rushed to her side. "Are you all right?"

Eyes glowing with excitement, Lauren said, "I'm better than fine. I'm great."

"I don't know whether to hug you or spank you," Rachel said.

"I'm sorry I went behind your back, but you and Dad wouldn't let me ride and I knew I could do it." Lauren shook her head, her pink hair drawing stares from several cowboys. "That was such a rush!"

Oh, Lord. After today, Clint was going to have his hands full steering Lauren away from bull riding. "How did you—"

"I told the woman at the check-in table that Dixie's replacement had a migraine and I was riding instead."

"Your dad's going to ground you for the rest of your life."

"Yeah, but it'll be worth it." Lauren hugged Rachel. When they broke apart, she said, "Let's cheer for Shannon."

"Ladies and gentlemen, Shannon Douglas is a local gal who's had a lot of success in women's bull riding. She won this event at both the Canyon City and Boot Hill Rodeos earlier in the summer." The fans applauded and a few waved signs with Shannon's name on them.

"Shannon's highest score to date is an 86, which she earned this past May at the Lane Frost Challenge Rodeo in Vernal, Utah." The JumboTron replayed the footage of Shannon's ride in Utah and the crowd stomped and hollered.

"If Shannon makes it to eight on Cracker Jack, she's got a good chance of beating Lauren McGraw's 82. Cracker Jack's a veteran bull. Let's see if Shannon can tame the beast!"

Shannon signaled to the gateman and Cracker Jack jumped for freedom. The bull was fast and strong, making Lauren's ride on Dancer look like a walk in the park. Shannon clung to her seat, even though the bull fought valiantly to throw her.

The buzzer rang and applause thundered through the stands. Clint and his partner closed in on the bull, but Shannon didn't need help. She leaped from Cracker Jack, stumbling once then sliding to a stop in the dirt before popping to her feet and running for the rails.

The JumboTron displayed an 85. "There you have it, folks! Shannon Douglas has taken the lead with an eighty-five!"

Rachel's chest swelled with pride as Shannon's friends congratulated her and Lauren. Because of these courageous women, Rachel had been able to increase the profits of her father's summer rodeos and maybe open the door for future women's bull-riding events.

"Next up is Skylar Riggins!"

Three more bull rides and a few more hours of rodeo and Rachel's job in Stagecoach, Arizona, would end.

"Uh-oh," Lauren mumbled to Rachel after the final ride. Clint marched in their direction. His stony expression didn't bode well for his daughter.

When Clint was ten feet away, Lauren said, "I can explain."

"No, you can't." Clint's angry gaze swept over Rachel and she opened her mouth to defend herself but he cut her off. "I know you didn't give Lauren permission to ride."

Rachel was relieved that, despite their personal situation, Clint trusted her to do right by his daughter.

"Dad, I'm sorry, but I had to prove I was ready to compete."

"You promised—"

"No." Lauren pointed a finger at Rachel. "She promised not to let me ride."

Clint's shoulders sagged.

Trying his damnedest to keep his emotions under control, he reined in his temper. He'd been wound tighter than a yo-yo since he'd climbed out of bed this morning. He hadn't gotten a wink of sleep the previous night. Visions of Rachel being stomped by a bull had kept him awake until the wee hours of the morning. Then he'd spent the hours leading up to the women's bull-riding event in a state of anxiety, terrified Rachel would be injured today.

When he'd heard his daughter's name over the loudspeaker his anxiety level had shot through the roof. Before he'd overcome the shock and put a stop to Lauren's antics, the chute had opened and she'd been in a battle for her life. Those eight seconds had lasted forever.

As he'd watched his daughter fight to keep her seat, his life had flashed through his mind. In that moment he'd decided that he needed to let go of the past and not allow his fear to control him.

"Mind if I speak with Lauren alone?" he asked.

Rachel walked off. Not caring that his eyes watered, he opened his arms and Lauren stepped into his embrace.

"I'm sorry, Dad. I won't ever disobey you again." Her sobs soaked the front of Clint's shirt.

Hugging her tight, he buried his face in her pink hair and for the first time confessed what had always been in his heart but he'd never had the courage to say. "I love you, honey."

"I love you, too." Lauren wiped her runny nose across the back of her hand. "It's not going to happen for a long time," she said. "But one of these days you'll have a great story to tell your grandchildren."

"You think?" Clint grinned.

Lauren joined Rachel and the other women and Clint stood by himself, pleased with how far he and Lauren had come this summer. His gaze swung to Rachel and the contentment turned into a heavy ache.

Clint needed to make a decision—one that was going to require a lot of strength and a leap of faith in himself.

Chapter Fourteen

"Hey, Dad." Lauren stepped inside the barn where Clint was mucking stalls. "What are you doing?"

"What does it look like I'm doing?" He pointed to an extra pitchfork against the wall. "Feel free to help."

Lauren plopped down on a hay bale near the stall. "What's got you so grouchy today?"

Not what...*who*. Three days had passed since the Piney Gorge Rodeo and Rachel was doing her best to avoid him. He'd had seventy-two hours of intense self-examination.

"Are you still mad at me for riding Dancer at the rodeo?"

"No, but I'll probably suffer nightmares of that ride the rest of my life."

His daughter chuckled then her expression sobered. "Dad."

"Huh?"

"I'm not going to ride any more bulls."

Clint stopped tossing hay into the wheelbarrow and stared.

"I don't regret competing in the rodeo because I proved to myself that I can do whatever I set my mind to."

His daughter's statement made Clint sad. "I've been a crappy father."

"I didn't make it very easy for you."

That was the truth but Clint refused to allow his daughter to accept any blame. "I should have been there for you more than I was."

Lauren jumped off the hay bale and hugged Clint.

He chuckled. "Does this mean you'll visit the ranch again?"

"Maybe." Lauren crinkled her nose. "I still hate the desert and no place compares to L.A., but I'd like to help with the rodeos next summer."

"I'm sure P.T. would love that." Spending the summers with his daughter was more than Clint deserved.

"What about Rachel? Are you guys going to stay together?"

Uncomfortable with the question, Clint returned to mucking. "What do you mean, stay together?"

"Uh-oh. Did you and Rachel fight?"

"No." Not really.

"What happened between you guys on the houseboat?"

Discussing matters of the heart—his in particular—with his daughter was off-limits. "That's private."

"I'm not asking if you two had sex."

Clint's face heated.

"Something went down on that boat because Rachel seemed really sad last night when I asked for her advice on hair color."

"You're getting rid of the pink?"

"I might switch to banana-yellow." Lauren waved her hand in the air. "Never mind that. I asked Rachel if she'd ever consider moving to Arizona, and she said even though she'd been born here it didn't feel like home."

"Have you spoken with Rachel today?"

"No. Her car's gone so I thought she went into town."

Panic surged through Clint. He flung the pitchfork aside.

"Where are you going?" Lauren followed him out of the barn.

Ignoring her question, Clint made a beeline to the main house, flung open the front door and marched down the hall to the guest bedroom. All Rachel's personal possessions were gone. He checked the closet—no suitcases. He went into the bathroom. No toothbrush. No cosmetic bag. He headed for the office. The top of the desk had been cleaned off.

Lauren poked her head around the door frame. "She left without saying goodbye."

Clint noticed a sheet of paper resting on the desk blotter. With a shaking hand he snatched up the note.

Dear Clint and Lauren,
Please forgive me for not saying good-bye in person but goodbyes make me sad. Lauren, thank you for your help with the rodeos. Because of your efforts with the media, the women's bull-riding events were a huge success. Good luck with your senior year of high school—I'll keep tabs on your progress through P.T. Clint, thank you for looking after my father all these years. You were there for him when I wasn't. Five Star Ranch will be in good hands with you at the helm.
Fondly,
Rachel

Had Rachel even considered how her sudden departure might affect P.T.'s health? Not to mention Clint's heart. A need to stop her propelled Clint into action. "Finish cleaning the stalls, will you?"

"Why?" Lauren ran outside after Clint.

"I'm heading to Phoenix." He dug his truck keys out of his jean pocket and cut across the ranch yard. Fearing he'd change his mind, he didn't take time to shower or throw on clean clothes.

Lauren stopped at the driver-side door. "Ask Rachel to stay, Dad."

He cranked the engine. "I can't promise she'll come back." He wanted Lauren to be prepared if he returned alone.

Lauren leaned through the open window. "Give P.T. a hug for me."

"I'll phone Mark Donner on the way out of town and ask him to stop by and check on the livestock."

Lauren grabbed Clint's sleeve before he shifted into Reverse. "Tell Rachel you love her, Dad. Say the words or she won't know how you really feel about her."

Did his daughter understand how much she was asking of him?

"Hey, Dad." Rachel stepped into the hospital room. P.T. waved her closer and she approached his bedside. Today her father appeared pale and thinner. "Did I catch you napping?"

"I don't take naps," he lied. His gaze swung

to the door. "Where's Clint? Didn't he come along?"

"No. He stayed at the ranch." After making the long drive to Phoenix, Rachel's courage had vanished. She hugged her father then drifted toward the window. "I have a confession to make," she said.

"Oh?"

"Before I come clean, did Mayor Ross phone you and chat about the Boot Hill Rodeo?" She faced her father.

"He left a message but I haven't returned his call."

"The mayor's considering the possibility of Five Star Rodeos promoting two events in one calendar year. A biannual schedule." Rachel smiled. "If Mayor Ross follows through with his idea then you know the other mayors will jump on board. You'll be back to a full rodeo schedule before you know it."

P.T. didn't appear impressed with the idea of expanding his business. After a moment, he said, "I'm waiting to hear your confession."

Rachel crossed her fingers behind her back. "I added an event to the rodeos this summer."

"What event?"

"Women's bull riding."

Instead of a curse word exploding from P.T.'s

mouth, he chuckled. Astonished, she said, "You knew, didn't you?"

His eyes twinkled.

"Who told you? Clint?"

"One of the radiology technicians rodeos on weekends. He entered the Canyon City Rodeo and bragged about the beautiful women riding bulls."

Wait until Clint learns P.T. knew all along. The thought saddened her that she'd have to share the news with Clint over the phone instead of in person.

Call him.

If she hadn't had the courage to say goodbye to Clint in person what made her believe speaking on the phone would be easier?

"What I can't figure out, Rachel, is how you got the mayors to sign on to a women's bull-riding event."

"It wasn't easy. The mayors considered me an outsider and didn't trust me."

"Outsider my arse. You're my daughter!"

"It would have helped if you'd told people you have a daughter." She quirked an eyebrow.

P.T.'s face flushed. Rachel came to his rescue.

"I asked Clint to pretend he was in charge of the rodeos, and when the mayors believed women's bull riding was Clint's idea they jumped on board."

"The hell you say." P.T. grabbed his phone. "Mitch, it's P.T. Hold on a minute." Rachel's father pushed a button on the phone then a moment later said, "Jack, it's P.T. I'm doing a three-way call. Don't hang up." A few seconds later… "John, P.T. here. I've got Mitch and Jack on the line with me."

Amused, Rachel swallowed a giggle.

"I hear you ignoramuses didn't believe I'd put my daughter in charge of the rodeos this summer." P.T. didn't give the mayors a chance to explain before he said, "You owe Rachel an apology." A pause. "That's right, it was Rachel's idea, not Clint's, to add the women's rough-stock event to the rodeo schedule." P.T. covered the phone with his hand and whispered, "They're debating how best to apologize…" P.T. cleared his throat. "A letter or a phone call will suffice." After a few short exchanges, P.T. disconnected the call.

"You never let on that you knew about the women's bull riding when we visited after the first rodeo," Rachel said.

"I asked you to run my business and I didn't want to interfere. Besides, when I'd heard how successful the rodeo was, I realized…"

"What?" she prodded.

"That I was old and stuck in my ways. I'd refused to consider adding a women's rough-stock event because—" P.T. stared unseeingly across the room.

"Because you blamed yourself for what happened to Mom."

His gaze shifted to Rachel and the depth of pain in his eyes sliced through her. If only he hadn't shoved her away years ago, they could have been a comfort to each other in dealing with her mother's death. Instead, her father had held the pain inside, allowing it to fester and weaken him. "I didn't want women competing partly because of your mother and partly because I was and still am old-fashioned."

"You mean a chauvinist?"

"I prefer old-fashioned."

"I'm relieved. The last thing I wanted to do was overstep my bounds."

"Your gamble paid off and put Five Star Rodeos back in the black." He cleared his throat. "I feel bad, though."

"Why?"

"Clint came to me with that idea a few years ago after the *Stagecoach Star* ran an article on Shannon Douglas trying to establish a women's bull-riding organization."

No wonder Clint had balked when she'd shared her idea with him. Even though she sympathized with the difficult position P.T. had put Clint in, Rachel wished with all her heart that

Clint had set aside his jealousy and had supported her efforts because he cared about her.

"Dad, I'm leaving for Rhode Island."

"Today?" Her father's face paled. "I expected you to stay until they released me from the clinic."

Did she dare confess she'd fallen in love with Clint and he'd broken her heart? That she was running from the future not the past? "I'd planned to, but…"

"But what? We haven't had a chance to talk. I'm sure you want to know more about your mother."

She inched closer to the bed. Learning why her father had sent her away after her mother had died eased some of the pain in Rachel's heart, but not all.

P.T. squeezed her hand. "Talk to me, daughter. Tell me what's in your heart."

"When you asked for my help, I imagined you'd missed me. Then I arrived and discovered that you'd taken Clint in and raised him as your son all the while ignoring me…" Tears burned her eyes. "It hurts, Dad," she whispered. "Really bad."

"When Clint came along I was a lonely, grumpy, angry man. I'd believed I'd ruined any chance at a relationship with you." P.T.'s eyes shone with tears. "I was afraid you'd reject me if I tried to become a part of your life. You were thriving with Edith and I told myself you didn't need me." He cleared his throat. "But Clint did need me."

"You took the coward's way out."

"I'm sorry, Rachel. I was wrong about so many things."

The apology Rachel had driven across the country for was hardly as satisfying as she'd anticipated.

"It's probably too late to ask this of you, but I've missed being your father. Please give me a second chance."

Rachel battled tears. "I have lots of questions about Mom," she whispered.

"I have plenty of stories to share about your mother." P.T. flashed a weak smile. "Will you reconsider and stay a few more weeks?"

"I need to prepare for another school year." Returning to the ranch where Clint lived would be too difficult for Rachel. "Maybe when you're feeling better you can fly out east and visit with me."

"Forget your job at the school. You've proven yourself, Rachel. I want you and Clint to run Five Star Rodeos."

"I worked hard to become a school psychologist. I'm good at what I do. I don't want to quit my job."

"Then apply for a position with the Yuma school district."

"Dad, I appreciate that you want us to grow closer but things are more complicated now than when I first arrived."

"What are you talking about?"

Tell him the truth. "I can't stay in Stagecoach because of Clint."

"I don't understand."

"The ranch is Clint's home, Dad. Not mine."

"But you're my daughter...my flesh and blood."

"That's right. Five Star Ranch is more your home, Rachel, than mine."

Rachel spun. Clint stood in the doorway—his clothes rumpled. His shirt covered with dry sweat stains. Pieces of straw stuck to his Stetson. He must have taken off as soon as he'd discovered she'd left. A warm, fuzzy feeling spread through her limbs as his soulful brown eyes pulled her into their depths sending her heart tumbling in a downward spiral.

This is why she'd left without saying goodbye—because Clint held her heart in the palm of his hand.

"I'll always be indebted to your father for taking me in." Clint looked at P.T. "You showed me how to be a man and you held my feet to the fire when I wanted to quit being a father."

Clint stepped farther into the room and shut the door behind him. "Not until you arrived at the ranch, Rachel, did I understand that I'd claimed something that wasn't mine to take—your father." He ignored P.T.'s gasp. "You were too nice to say it but we both knew I wanted to see you fail, Rachel. I wanted to show P.T. that I was the better person to run Five Star Rodeos." The pain in Clint's eyes was so clear that it hurt Rachel to meet his gaze. "The thought of losing the only home I'd ever felt comfortable in...ever felt wanted...scared me to death."

He swallowed hard. "Not until you came into my life did I realize what I'd refused to acknowledge. P.T. was the only person who'd made me feel worthy. Made me feel as if I mattered. That I counted on this earth. Over time, I'd allowed my self-worth to be defined by P.T.'s acceptance.

"Then I fell in love with you." Clint took a step toward Rachel but pulled up short.

Rachel's heart thundered. Her courage weakened and the voice in her head demanded to know how she could walk away from a man like Clint. Loving him wouldn't be easy, neat or rational. In fact, her summer with the cowboy proved the experience would be tough, messy and insane.

But gloriously exciting and fulfilling.

"You turned out to be everything I thought you weren't—kind, caring, loving, brave." Clint's gaze pierced Rachel. "You made me see that a home is more than a location or a pillow to rest my head on at night or place to cook a meal and take a shower."

"You think I'm brave?" No one had ever paid her such a compliment.

"Yes, brave, but not because you rode a bull. Because you answered your father's call when you believed he didn't love you. You had the courage to give P.T. a second chance."

"What's this about riding a bull?" P.T. bellowed. "Is that how you really broke your fingers?"

"Yes," Rachel said, never taking her eyes off Clint.

"By God, daughter, if you ever do such a stupid thing again, I'll—"

"Be quiet, P.T.," Clint said. "I love you, Rachel. And I know I have P.T.'s blessing when I ask you this. Please marry me and make our family complete. P.T., Lauren and especially me, well, we need you."

Tears burned Rachel's eyes. She'd never believed in a million years that returning to her birthplace would in fact be returning home.

"Well, daughter. Are you going to marry Clint?"

"You can do better than me, Rachel," Clint said. "I may not be the man of your dreams or all that easy to live with, but I promise you won't find a man more loyal than me who will love you the rest of your life and stand by your side through good times and bad." Clint swept a strand of hair off her cheek. "Please stay."

"I love you, Clint." Rachel flung her arms around his neck and squeezed. "Yes, I'll marry you. Yes, I'll move back to Five Star Ranch. No, I won't run Five Star Rodeos, but I will help out on occasion." She smiled at P.T. "And yes, I will give my father a second chance."

A tear escaped P.T.'s eye. "Daughter, if there is anyone who deserves a loving family of their own it's you."

She hugged her father. "I love you, Dad."

"I've always loved you, Rachel, even though I failed to show you." He pointed his finger at Clint. "You make her happy, son, or you'll answer to me."

"Yes, sir."

"I'm tired. You two go celebrate with a nice dinner while I rest."

"We'll stop at the hospital before we leave town." Rachel kissed P.T.'s forehead.

As soon as she and Clint left the room and closed the door behind them, Clint pressed her against the corridor wall. "Damn it, Rachel. When you drove away this morning with your car packed and no goodbye, you ripped my heart from my chest."

"I left you a note." Lord, she hoped Clint would always steal her breath—even twenty years from now.

"I'm a lot like P.T. I don't know how to show people I care about them. I started falling in love with you when Curly stopped your prissy car in the middle of the road."

"But then you found out I was P.T.'s daughter—"

"And you scared me to death. P.T.'s been the only person who's stuck by me. I didn't want to lose him but you changed all that."

"How?"

"You made me believe in myself and believe I was worthy of love."

"What would you have done if I'd turned down your proposal?" she asked.

"I would have moved on. Found work at another ranch." He kissed the corner of her mouth. "And thanks to you I would have been okay. I would have survived."

"So you don't need me as much as you believe."

"No. I need you more than I'd ever imagined possible. You're the sweetness, the color, the warmth that's been missing from my life.

You make me whole." He nuzzled her temple. "I love you, Rachel. Please grow old with me."

"You're sure?"

"More sure than I've ever been about anything, including P.T.'s love for me."

"I'm glad, because I really didn't know how I was going to walk away from you, my father and Lauren without being miserable the rest of my life."

"You're a city girl. If you don't want to live on the ranch, I'll move to Rhode Island."

Rachel's heart melted at Clint's offer, but she wanted to spend as much time with her father as possible in case he didn't beat his cancer. She also believed moving to Arizona would allow her and her father to continue to mend their relationship, as well as make Rachel feel closer to her mother.

Grasping Clint's hand, she said, "Let's go home."

Rachel had come full circle and this time she was home for good and no one and nothing on earth could make her leave.

* * * * *

REQUEST YOUR FREE BOOKS!

2 FREE NOVELS PLUS 2 FREE GIFTS!

LARGER-PRINT BOOKS!

**GET 2 FREE
LARGER-PRINT NOVELS
PLUS 2 FREE
MYSTERY GIFTS**

Love Inspired®
SUSPENSE

RIVETING INSPIRATIONAL ROMANCE

Larger-print novels are now available...

YES! Please send me 2 FREE LARGER-PRINT Love Inspired® Suspense novels and my 2 FREE mystery gifts (gifts are worth about $10). After receiving them, if I don't wish to receive any more books, I can return the shipping statement marked "cancel". If I don't cancel, I will receive 4 brand-new novels every month and be billed just $4.99 per book in the U.S. or $5.49 per book in Canada. That's a saving of at least 23% off the cover price. It's quite a bargain! Shipping and handling is just 50¢ per book in the U.S. and 75¢ per book in Canada.* I understand that accepting the 2 free books and gifts places me under no obligation to buy anything. I can always return a shipment and cancel at any time. Even if I never buy another book, the two free books and gifts are mine to keep forever.

110/310 IDN FEH3

Name	(PLEASE PRINT)	
Address		Apt. #
City	State/Prov.	Zip/Postal Code

Signature (if under 18, a parent or guardian must sign)

Mail to the **Reader Service:**
IN U.S.A.: P.O. Box 1867, Buffalo, NY 14240-1867
IN CANADA: P.O. Box 609, Fort Erie, Ontario L2A 5X3

Not valid for current subscribers to Love Inspired Suspense larger-print books.

**Are you a current subscriber to Love Inspired Suspense books
and want to receive the larger-print edition?
Call 1-800-873-8635 or visit www.ReaderService.com.**

* Terms and prices subject to change without notice. Prices do not include applicable taxes. Sales tax applicable in N.Y. Canadian residents will be charged applicable taxes. Offer not valid in Quebec. This offer is limited to one order per household. All orders subject to credit approval. Credit or debit balances in a customer's account(s) may be offset by any other outstanding balance owed by or to the customer. Please allow 4 to 6 weeks for delivery. Offer available while quantities last.

Your Privacy—The Reader Service is committed to protecting your privacy. Our Privacy Policy is available online at www.ReaderService.com or upon request from the Reader Service.

We make a portion of our mailing list available to reputable third parties that offer products we believe may interest you. If you prefer that we not exchange your name with third parties, or if you wish to clarify or modify your communication preferences, please visit us at www.ReaderService.com/consumerschoice or write to us at Reader Service Preference Service, P.O. Box 9062, Buffalo, NY 14269. Include your complete name and address.

LISUSLP11B